Funny Stories
Ten Year Olds

Helen Paiba is known as one of the most committed, knowledgeable and acclaimed children's booksellers in Britain. For more than twenty years she owned and ran the Children's Bookshop in Muswell Hill, London, which under her guidance gained a superb reputation for its range of children's books and for the advice available to its customers.

Helen was involved with the Booksellers Association for many years and served on both its Children's Bookselling Group and the Trade Practices Committee. In 1995 she was given honorary life membership of the Booksellers Association of Great Britain and Ireland in recognition of her outstanding services to the association and to the book trade. In the same year the Children's Book Circle (sponsored by Books for Children) honoured her with the Eleanor Farjeon Award, given for distinguished service to the world of children's books.

She retired in 1995 and now lives in London.

Funny
STORIES
for Ten Year Olds

COMPILED BY HELEN PAIBA

ILLUSTRATED BY JUDY BROWN

MACMILLAN
CHILDREN'S BOOKS

First published 2000 by Macmillan Children's Books
a division of Macmillan Publishers Limited
25 Eccleston Place, London SW1W 9NF
Basingstoke and Oxford
www.macmillan.co.uk

Associated companies throughout the world

ISBN 0 330 39127 5

1 3 5 7 9 8 6 4 2

A CIP catalogue record for this book is available
from the British Library.

Typeset by SX Composing DTP, Rayleigh, Essex
Printed and bound in Great Britain by
Mackays of Chatham plc, Kent

Contents

Fun Run   1
ROBERT LEESON

Murder by Omelette   22
HAZEL TOWNSON

Burglars!   34
NORMAN HUNTER

Barker   46
PETER DICKINSON

The Man with the Silver Tongue   65
RORY MCGRATH

Double Bluff   80
HELEN CRESSWELL

Jekyll and Jane   89
TERRANCE DICKS

William's Busy Day   98
RICHMAL CROMPTON

Sniff Finds a Seagull   139
IAN WHYBROW

A Work of Art   148
MARGARET MAHY

The Day I Died   164
TERRY TAPP

You Can't Bring That in Here   193
ROBERT SWINDELLS

Sticky Bun and the Sandwich Challenge   200
JANET FRANCES SMITH

Mystery Tour   213
JAN MARK

The Horrible Story   238
MARGARET MAHY

Fun Run

Robert Leeson

There are three of us – Scott, built like an ape, Adrian, like a famine victim, and me – neat and medium sized.

Scott's mad. He does things first, then thinks afterwards. Adrian worries. He wouldn't do anything for fear of getting into trouble – if it weren't for Scott.

And they'd both be lost without me. I think things out. I have the ideas. It sounds big-headed to say I'm the brains, but, in all modesty, I am.

Take the Fun Run, the school's big outdoor event of the year. Naturally they wait till winter's coming on and it's getting cold and they send you off in PE kit, half-naked, running miles up hill and down dale. If you don't get lost or fall off a hill, you crawl in plastered in mud and suffering from hypothermia, to find all the hot water's been used by idiots who got in first. And they laugh at you. They stand there fully dressed and laugh as you stagger in. That's why they call it a fun run.

And the final insult, it's all for charity.

"The Homeless this year," said Mr Hipwell, PE thug-in-chief. "This year we aim to beat last year's total and go over the seven hundred pound mark. Get your sponsor sheets from the office."

"See the way he was grinning," I told Scott and Adrian. "He's a sadist. Imagine him in jackboots. He doesn't care about the Homeless. He just wants to see us suffer."

"Yer," said Scott sticking his jaw out. "He can stuff his Fun Run."

"Oh, you can't say that," Adrian began to look worried.

"Hang about," I took charge. "We've got to box clever." I thought for a minute. "He's got no right to make us, has he? I mean this is supposed to be charity. I bet it's . . ." I had a sudden inspiration. "I bet it's not in the National Curriculum. And, if it's not, this is illegal."

They were listening.

"My dad reckons this charity business is a con. The government ought to help the homeless. Little bits of fund-raising only make matters worse."

Well, my dad hadn't said anything about the Fun Run, but if he had, that's what he'd have said. I know the way his mind works.

Scott's eyes glazed over. They always do when things get complicated. But Adrian's more intelligent. He looked worried.

"So?" said Scott.

"So we go to Hippo and we tell him we're not going. It's voluntary. We don't believe in charity – on principle. And it's outside the National Curriculum."

"But I do," murmured Adrian.

"Do what?"

"Believe in charity. I put my spare pennies in a box for – things." He looked sad. "I saw this programme on the box, people living in cardboard shelters."

"Shut up," we both said. Scott turned to me. "OK, we go and see Hippo and you do the talking."

"He'll get mad at us," worried Adrian.

He was right. Hipwell looked at me from a great height. He ignored the others and seemed to think it was all my idea.

"Underneath that convoluted claptrap about charity," he bellowed, "you have the soul of a wood louse . . ."

He put his large ugly face close to mine and hissed. "I don't care what your father thinks. I don't care what the Secretary of State for Education thinks. I do not care about your consciences, collective or individual. The Fun Run is compulsory. You, you and you are going to take part and you are going to enjoy it, whether you like it or not."

Afterwards for some reason the others were cool towards me. But next day, Scott brightened up.

"I've cracked it. We wag off."

"We'll get caught," agonized Adrian.

"Not if we box clever," I took charge. "My dad reckons that when our school was the Grammar and they used to call it the Cross Country, they used to sneak off down Hangman's Lane. Then they hung about in Brookfield Park while the others ran the full course. They were smart. They didn't join in at the front, but halfway like."

"Right." Now Scott tried to take charge. He's got this thing about being a leader and he hasn't the intellect. "We do that." He stuck his finger in my chest. "You work out the details." Then he thumped Adrian on the back and made him swallow his Dental Health chewing gum. "Don't fret. It'll be a doddle."

Well, it wasn't. Hippo ran the first mile with us. He wanted to enjoy seeing us struggle up the hill out of town. You could see people looking at us as we staggered past, muttering about life support and other witty remarks. It was very embarrassing.

What made it worse was the other two. Adrian kept saying, "My mum says I shouldn't run uphill,

it's bad for my chest." And Scott kept asking, "Where's Hangman's Lane?"

Was it my fault the whole area had been changed since my dad's day?

"They must have renamed it."

Scott glared at me. "Right. The moment Hippo goes ahead we slip off that way." He jerked his head towards the left.

After twenty agonizing minutes when I thought my legs would crumple, Hippo got tired of monitoring us and shot off ahead.

"Now," muttered Scott. Suddenly he started to hop. "Oh me . . . foot," he gasped and staggered out of the ruck. I did the same. Adrian followed us, blushing red and not having the nerve to fake a stone in his sock.

"Right. Lead the way to Brookfield," Scott told me.

I looked round. There were houses everywhere, all the same. None of the roads led anywhere. How did people find their way?

"This way," I said quickly and set off with the others trailing behind. One road led into another, more houses, more gardens. No shops, no bus stops. No people. We walked for ten minutes.

Scott stopped. "You're lost."

I shrugged. "So are you."

Scott raised his hands as if he was going to put

them round my throat, then he said, "Let's ask somebody."

Adrian looked horrified as Scott marched up a garden path and banged on a door. No answer. Next door was the same. At last, after the fourth try, Scott came back to the road.

"Let's hitch," he said.

"Oh no," Adrian was alarmed. "You don't know who it'll be."

"Get off," Scott snapped. He turned and signalled and to my amazement, a car pulled up. A man with a red face and ginger moustache looked out.

"Whither bound?"

There was something funny about his manner, but I thought quickly and spoke before Scott could muck things up.

"We're on an initiative test, sir." That seemed to please him. At least he started to grin. "We have to get to Brookfield Park by two fifteen exactly."

"By car?"

"That's it. Any mode of transport, sir. The main thing is initiative. We get points for being there, not for distance . . ."

"Sounds like cheating to me," growled the driver. "Still, times change. Hop in the back."

We climbed into the back of the car and off he went like the clappers, throwing us over one another.

"I think we've made a mistake, taking a lift from a stranger," Adrian whispered.

"Shut up," we told him. I turned to Scott. "See, we'll be there in five minutes."

"We're going the wrong way," whispered Adrian.

"How d'you make that out?"

"He's going uphill. School's downhill."

"Ah, you worry too much. He's getting back on the main road." I started to chat up the driver. "Very good of you to help us, sir."

"Huh," he grunted. "Initiative test, eh? In my day we didn't go in for that sort of rubbish. Too much like skiving. We had the Cross Country. Great times, those. Up to the top of the valley round along the ridge to the beacon, then down through the woods."

"Did you come in first, sir?"

"Ha, first five. Nothing less worthwhile. We always knew when we got to that park down by the market square that we were on the last lap."

"That's right, not far from school, sir." I felt Scott nudge me but ignored him.

"Right," said the driver, "quarter of a mile. That's where the skivers used to hang about and try and join in. Of course we never let them get ahead. Little turds. Not likely."

The car swerved round another corner. Now we were in a country lane, climbing steeply.

8

Adrian cleared his throat. "Excuse me, sir, but I think you're going the wrong way."

"Ha," snorted the driver. "You think so. Well I'm not. I'm taking you young slugs back to the Cross Country route. I'm going to see you don't get away with it. Cheek," he muttered.

The situation was dodgy. Some finesse was called for.

"Just drop us here if you like, sir," I said. "Wouldn't be fair to take us right up to where the rest are. We'll catch them up."

He swung round and glowered while the car waltzed to and fro across the white line.

"Don't try your smarm on me, boy. I'm taking you to the halfway mark so you don't sneak back. You're going to finish the course – like men."

Suddenly Scott wound down the window on his side and stuck out his head. "Help, help," he yelled. "This dirty old man's abducting us."

It was so crude, I was ashamed. Adrian had almost vanished into the seat, his face crimson. My head banged against the seat in front as the car stopped dead.

"Out," ordered the driver. "I might have known."

We tumbled out on to the grass verge.

"No sporting spirit – typical," he snarled as the car shot up off the road.

We looked at each other then down into the valley. Town and school looked miles away.

"Come on," said Scott, crossing the road.

"Where're you going?" I demanded.

"Over here." Scott launched himself at the stone wall beside the road.

Adrian was still worried. "We'll get lost."

"Impossible. Downhill all the way."

It was. There was a big sloping field, then trees, then another wall, more grass, soft and slippery. We ran, we tripped, we tumbled, we rolled over and over. We couldn't stop, through grass clumps, thistles, gorse bushes and cowpats, till, hysterical with laughing, we shot over a little cliff and landed in a stream.

"My mum said I shouldn't get wet," moaned Adrian.

"You'll dry off," said Scott. "Come on, follow the stream down. Bound to lead to the river."

We followed, down the stream bed, from one field to another, dodging under bridges, barbed wire, going down, down. Till suddenly a big green bank loomed and the stream vanished.

"We're stuck," said Adrian. "We'll have to go back."

"Give over," jeered Scott. "There's a culvert."

There was too, at the bottom of the bank, a brick

tunnel about a metre or so high. The stream poured into the dark and it smelt like death.

"We'll get our feet wet."

"You won't. Listen. My brother told me. You walk sideways and put your hands on the opposite side. Like this."

Swiftly, like a crab, Scott disappeared into the gloom. I followed again, and after a bit of mither, so did Adrian. Five minutes later, a bit wet round the edges where we'd slipped on the slimy brickwork, we got out into daylight.

"Look at that!"

In front was a broad green hollow. On one side blackberry bushes climbed the slope, thick with dark berries. On the other there were chestnut trees, dripping conkers. We forgot what we were supposed to be doing, even Adrian, and charged down. We stuffed ourselves with berries and filled our pockets with big, glossy conkers.

We'd have stopped all afternoon, but we were interrupted.

"Hey. You lads!"

Back at the top of the bank over the culvert was a bloke. A big bloke, with a dog, bigger than himself.

"You lot. Come here."

Adrian went pale. "I told you we'd get into trouble."

It was time for me to take charge. I shouted to the man. "We're not doing any damage."

Even at that distance I could see his face go deep red.

"You're trespassing, you—" and a number of words followed. The sort you get told off for using in the school yard.

I answered quite reasonably. Dad had told me all about the law of trespass. "We'll leave by the shortest route."

"— — — —," he yelled. Then he let the dog go.

We went down the slope like rockets. Adrian was well in front. Behind us I could hear the dog rasping away like the Hound of the Baskervilles. And I didn't have my service revolver. The wall up at the top of the hollow must have been two metres high but Scott and I went over it like swallows, carrying Adrian with us.

"I've cut me knee," he howled.

We crashed down on the other side, rolled down a bank and into the road.

"Look at those boys. The things they get up to," said a voice.

We looked round. We were in the main road, and cars were charging round us, hooting. Behind us was a bus stop, a broken-down shelter and a bench with three fat women, carrying shopping bags. One of

them burst out laughing.

"Joe Stanley's been after you with his dog."

She nudged her neighbours and they laughed as well. Then one called, "Hey up. Here's t'bus."

Swinging into the space by the shelter came the little bus with the beautiful words on the indicator: *Hadleigh Market Place.*

Already the women were clambering up the steps. Scott was right behind them. Adrian hung back.

"We've not got the fare."

"Don't worry," I assured him. "We just give our addresses."

The driver looked funny. "How do I know it's your address?" he demanded.

I was firm. "You're forced to accept it, it's the law."

He fixed me with his eye. "Any more of that, me lad and your name'll be Walker."

"Oh, come on Harold," said one of the women. "We'll pay for 'em, won't we girls? I can take one child free on me warrant."

The driver scowled. "All right. That's one."

"I'll do another," said the second woman. "I'll have the skinny one with the cut knee. He can come and sit with me, poor love."

"I'll have the big 'un," said the third. "He looks cheeky."

"Well, I'll have the one that's left," said the first woman. "He's not up to much but he'll do. Come here lad," she told me and patted the seat, well about a quarter of it that was left, beside her.

The bus pulled out into the road and we rolled down into Hadleigh. We were silent, but the women talked all the way.

"What are you lot up to then?" A nudge in my ribs, that nearly sent me into the gangway, told me I was supposed to answer.

I started my spiel about the initiative test, but they all laughed like drains.

"Get off with your bother. You've been on the Fun Run and got tired. My grandson tapped me for fifty pence for it."

"Well, you can't blame the poor little jiggers," said my sponsor, scoring a centre against my ribs with her elbow. "I didn't reckon much to sports when I were a girl."

"My mum," announced the second woman, "wouldn't let me go in for outdoor sports at school – 'cause of my health."

The others shrieked for some reason.

"You made up for lost time when you left school," they called. The driver looked round and winked.

"That were indoor sports."

"You shut up, Harold," they all howled together as the bus drove into Hadleigh and swung into the bus station by the market. The women, still cackling, rolled away across the square. I turned to Adrian and Scott.

"What did I tell you? I fixed that all right."

But Adrian wasn't happy yet. "How we going to get back to school?"

"Easy, quarter of a mile up the road."

"Yes, but all the kids coming down for the buses'll see us. Look they're coming in now. Hey, we aren't half late."

He was right. School was well over and first years were streaming into the bus station.

"Round here," said Scott. "There's a bench. We can wait while they go."

There was a seat around the corner of the station caff.

"There's someone there," complained Adrian.

"Plenty of room," I replied. But that wasn't strictly true.

Sitting in the middle of the bench was an old dosser. Well, he looked old with his beard flowing over his chest. An ancient raincoat stiff with dirt like a cloak covered most of him, except for the frayed trouser ends and broken boots. Plastic bags and boxes took up most of the rest of the seat.

I was just going to ask him politely to make room when the smell from him hit me. I felt dizzy. No wonder there was no one else sitting there. We couldn't sit down, but we couldn't move off in case the school bus crowd saw us.

"What're you gawping at?"

The voice came from inside the beard.

"Er, nothing."

"Well, clear off then."

"We've as much right to stay here as you," I said with dignity.

The shape on the bench straightened up. Two bloodshot eyes glowed like lamps. A face came into view.

"You've got homes, haven't you? What d'you want to pester me for? Shove off."

"In a minute, when the crowd clears," I said.

His eyes clouded over. But his forehead got all ridged. It looked as though he were thinking. But I couldn't be sure. Then his shoulders began to shake up and down, till the whole body under the dirty mac was quivering. From the middle of the whiskers came a choking gasping sound. For a moment I thought he was having a fit. Then I realized he was laughing. Next minute he started to wheeze and cough like an old car breaking down. Then he spoke.

"I know what you're up to. You wagged off the Cross. Hey, come and sit down." He started to shift his gear and, feeling slightly sick, we sat down. Scott managed to sit farthest away. Adrian and I felt as if we were wrapped in a blanket of pong. The old dosser tapped me on the knee.

"We used to. We did all we could to get out of games. We used to pick the spot, go over the wall, lie on the grass or pick berries then get the bus back. There were always somebody soft-hearted who'd pay us fares. Don't suppose it'd work now. Folk are too selfish."

He gripped my knee. His face turned to mine and his foul breath made me feel queasy.

"It would have been less bother to go on the Cross Country, 'cause we were worn out when we got back. But that never occurred to us. But one year we overdid it."

17

His voice died. I thought he'd gone to sleep, but he was thinking: "One year we nipped off down Hangmans Lane to Brookfield Park, then joined in and came first. That did it. We all got six strokes. Don't suppose they use the cane these days. Country's going to the dogs . . ."

"Hey mister," said Scott. "When you came back on the bus how did you get into school without folk seeing you?"

The dosser was spurred into action. He lumbered to his feet, scooped up his gear, and lurched towards the tarred fence behind the bus garage. We stared, then followed him. When we caught up he'd pushed back two planks and was forcing his way through.

Beyond the fence was waste ground. Old houses and workshops had been flattened and left. Rank grass, bushes, small trees had grown up between the brickpiles. A trail of smoke rose behind a half-demolished wall. Here and there in corners of old buildings, slabs of board, old doors and sheets of iron and plastic had been used to make shelters. There must have been a dozen of them. People were living here.

In the shelter of the wall was a fire, a litter of bags, boxes, cans. And around the fire a dozen men and women. As we followed the dosser, a man got up from the fireside and swore at us. But our man stopped him.

"They're with me," he grunted. The rest glared at us but said nothing.

Now we were over the waste ground and ahead I could see the river. Directly below us was an old lock, water gushing through the broken gates. The tramp pointed. Across the water was more waste ground, then a hedge, and over the top of the hedge in the distance we could see goal posts and the roof of school.

"Back way in. Over the field and across to the gym. No one ever found out."

Adrian thanked him. He looked at us without speaking. I felt I should say something.

"Our cross-country. It was a Fun Run – for the Homeless."

His shoulders started to quiver again, the lines of his face disappeared and he coughed and choked. Then he found his voice.

"Wait till I tell 'em. No wonder you wagged off."

The awful grating sound started again. We didn't wait now but ran across the lock. Light was fading but I could see him standing there.

Scott peered ahead. "Waste of time going back to school. I bet it's all locked up over there. Nobody about. I'm off home."

"Like this?" squealed Adrian pointing to his mud-spattered running gear.

19

"Dah. Who's going to see?" Scott turned to me. "We can nip round the side and climb over the gate."

I was thinking, working out a number of convincing lines I could take when I got home: lost way, abducted by mad pervert, stopped to help old ladies on bus, Task Force visit to Hadleigh's Cardboard City. They all seemed tempting.

"I'll get skinned if I go home like this," said Adrian. "I'm going to the gym."

"It'll be shut up."

"Might not."

"Will."

Adrian's face suddenly changed. "For once, just once will you two do something I say?"

With that he started over the field, and without thinking Scott and I followed. I realized how stiff and tired I was. As we reached the gym, Adrian signalled excitedly.

"Open," he whispered. "They must have forgotten."

We sneaked in, heading for the changing room. But as we pushed open the inner door, the lights went on. We blinked in the glare as the room filled with a tremendous noise. It was packed with kids and teachers all laughing, pointing, clapping. Someone started to chant:

"Why were you born so beautiful?"

Why were you born at all?"

I turned to Adrian. I was going to tell him what I thought of his brilliant idea when Hipwell raised his meaty hand.

"All right, all right. A bit of hush please." Then to us. "Congratulations. No one has ever been one hour sixteen minutes late before."

Cheering started. Scott grinned sheepishly. Adrian was one big blush.

"We had the ingenious idea of having a sweepstake. How late would you be? Denny Harris won and he agreed to put the money back in the kitty. That means you three have raised thirty-seven pounds and twelve pence for the Fun Run and you come top of the list. Congratulations."

More applause. Scott started to laugh. Adrian sniggered. I couldn't think of anything to say, so I joined in.

Murder by Omelette

Hazel Townson

Of course, I didn't really mean to kill our Clarissa; it was just that Fate seemed to lead me on that way. Not that I hadn't plenty of motive, mostly supplied by my mum.

"You should be proud of your sister," Mum told me nine million times a day. But why should I be proud because my big sister came top of the class every term; was elected head prefect; starred in the school play; captained the unconquered hockey team; played first flute in the school orchestra; broke twenty hearts a week, and thoroughly cramped my style? As if that wasn't enough, she'd now been chosen as the next Carnival Queen.

"Clarissa Walters, Carnival Queen! Just imagine!"

My mother's face went all dreamy – and so did mine. But whereas Mum was seeing metres of tulle and satin topped by a shining crown, I was seeing deadly arrows, poison bottles, yawning traps and boiling whirlpools. I suppose it was jealousy really, but I couldn't help it, any more than I could help being freckled, forgetful, clumsy-footed, tone deaf, plain dumb, and no ladykiller. In fact, to take that last bit both ways, I'd never even thought of killing a lady before; I'm not a violent lad as a rule. But it just so happened that the very next day we had poisonous toadstools at school. (For a nature lesson, not for school dinner, surprise, surprise!)

I was amazed at how many different kinds of poisonous toadstools there were. Some of them looked almost like real mushrooms. In fact, it seemed incredible that we'd all lived this long.

Mrs Blair, our teacher, took us out into Craydon Woods to identify some, and it turned out that the deadliest were quite good-looking, just like people.

"It's important for you to know the difference," Mrs Blair explained, "then there's no chance of your being poisoned. See! – those are the ones you must never pick. Georgie Walters, are you listening?"

Fair comment; I wasn't taking all that much notice. I hated any kind of nature study and always came bottom of the class in a test so I figured there wasn't much point in listening too hard. But as it happens I HAD heard that bit, and when I got left behind – through deliberate moody dawdling – I suddenly found myself dragging a crumpled old paper bag out of my pocket and filling it with poisonous toadstools . . . "the ones you must never pick".

I must have been mad! Goodness knew what I was going to do with them – although I have a fair reputation at our house for turning out a snazzy omelette; my one and only success in life. I stuffed the bag into my pocket and ran. Sweating with guilt, I caught up with the others and spent the rest of the day in a rather nasty blur.

A murderer in the family! What would it do to my dad's Masonic chances, Mum's cake-stall at the annual church fête or Gran's running battle to be

boss of our local Meals-on-Wheels? To say nothing of the victim, ". . . this lovely young genius, cruelly cut down in the flower of her youth . . ." No marks for guessing who'd get all the sympathy, the eulogies, the glory everlasting. No, no; this wouldn't do at all.

And yet somehow I couldn't get rid of those toadstools. Three times I tried to stuff them into one of the school dustbins, but at the last minute my hand always drew back again, still clutching the bag as if my palm were oozing glue.

When I got home I tried our dustbin with the same result, then decided instead to hide the bag of toadstools in a good, safe place until I came unstuck (psychologically, that is). This was a big mistake, for it preyed on my mind. That night I had a hideous nightmare in which I served up for my sister a delicious-looking poisoned "mushroom" omelette which Clarrie, with a sinister grin, refused to taste. She passed it over to Mum and Dad instead, and after only one bite each they both toppled down from their chairs, stone-dead.

Then, with an even more sinister grin, Clarrie tried to make me eat what was left. She was actually poking forkfuls of it into my yelling mouth when I woke in a blind panic vowing to get rid of those toadstools at once. Burn them; bury them; bowl them out to sea.

But they'd gone! Disappeared!

I couldn't find them anywhere!

In fact, after that mind-boggling dream, I couldn't even be sure by now where my good, safe hiding place had been. Shaking with dread, I emptied every pocket, shelf and drawer. I stripped my bed. I shunted the furniture around. I rolled back the rugs. I turned my room inside out and upside down. I even took a frantic trowel to the window-box on my sill and climbed, at risk of life and limb, on to the dusty wardrobe top. But those toadstools in their tatty paper bag were nowhere to be seen. Had I sleep-walked and moved them? Had someone stolen into my room in the middle of the night and taken them? Or, last shred of hope, did that horrible nightmare begin with me bringing those toadstools home? Perhaps they were still in my desk at school?

Breakfastless, I cycled off to school in a frenzy of hope – but no toadstools! Not in my desk; not in my football locker; not even in the lost property office.

Of course, I didn't dare make too many enquiries, but I put in plenty of detective work. I tracked down every paper bag in the building – and some of their contents were pretty disgusting, I can tell you! – but I might as well have saved myself the risk of bubonic plague.

How I struggled through the day I shall never

know. It was the longest day in living memory – if you could call this living – punctuated by the concern of those who thought I had either been bewitched, sniffed glue behind the bike-shed or become the youngest-ever victim of *senile dementia*. Only the final bell could bring me back to life and set me cycling off in another sudden frenzy in case there was somewhere at home that I'd forgotten to search.

There was another further terrible shock in store.

When I reached home, I found to my horror that we were having mushroom pie for supper!

"Our Clarrie made it in cookery class," Mum explained. "Doesn't it look delicious? You know, our Georgie, you should be proud of your sister; she'll make someone a dead clever wife one day."

"Dead, maybe! Or at least, deadly," I thought, but I hadn't time to argue. As Mum placed Clarrie's pie in the oven my brain was whizzing round, wondering where those mushrooms had come from. Clarrie must have taken them from home this morning. FROM THIS VERY HOUSE! So was my clever sister turning the tables on me? Was my hideous nightmare about to come true?

I dithered around in an ague of anxiety until my anxiously flapping ears learned how Clarrie had that morning shrieked with horror, having forgotten to buy the mushrooms for her recipe. Luckily for her, or so she thought, Mum had happened to find some in the fridge.

"Quite a surprise it was. I guess Dad must have picked them when he took the dog out early yesterday morning."

But of course Dad hadn't. It was obvious that after years of brainwashing I had hygienically, if absentmindedly, put them in the fridge myself. Or else someone had discovered my hiding place and moved them for me.

"Criminal negligence!" the judge would call it.

Well, of course I had to stop that pie being eaten. Should I confess? Or snatch it from the oven and make off with it?

Wait a minute, though, no need to be hasty! Maybe I could sort this thing out without throwing suspicion on myself after all. Just suppose that pie turned out to be uneatable . . .?

When no one was looking I turned up the oven temperature as high as it would go.

Mum was the first to smell burning but it was already too late, because I'd been diverting her attention to non-existent strange noises in the airing-cupboard. By the time she had dashed back to the kitchen and opened the oven door a great cloud of smoke was waiting to whoosh out.

"Oh, Clarrie!" she wailed. "Your lovely pie!"

I sulked in a corner, bracing myself for the storm.

Clarrie was certainly annoyed, though not in the way I expected.

"Oh, Mum! You were never going to make us eat that pie! I TOLD you it was no good! I only brought it home for the dog."

"Modest, as usual!" Mum tossed a supercilious smile in my direction. "Our Clarrie never brags, though if anybody's got good cause to brag, it's her. And see how considerate she is of other people? Trying not to make me feel bad for letting her pie get burnt! You know, our Georgie, I wish you'd take a leaf out of your sister's book and learn a few refinements. You should be—"

"proud of your sister!" I finished for her, mockingly.

"Well, you needn't be proud of my cookery," snapped Clarrie. "It's not my thing at all."

It turned out that their cookery teacher had warned Clarrie the pie would taste terrible because she had missed out some vital ingredient. That wasn't the first time, either.

"You know very well I'm no good at cookery, Mum. (You can't have forgotten that terrible swiss roll!) So I don't know why you have to keep on pretending I'm so marvellous. Everybody has at least one thing they just can't do, and that's mine. I specially told you not to try eating that pie but you wouldn't take any notice. Look, if you were relying on that for supper, why don't we get our Georgie to make us one of his super omelettes?"

WHAT? Had I heard aright? Could this be praise? From my larger-than-life big sister?

It could!

Our Clarrie had actually admitted there was something I could do better than she could!

All of a sudden, I felt positively radiant. Why, I loved that girl! She was the best sister a guy ever had. You just needed to spend a little time getting to know her, that was all. She was a person of high intelligence and impeccable judgement.

"Right!" I declared. "I'll make you the best

omelette you've ever tasted – or ever will taste in the whole of your lives."

As I reached for the mixing-bowl, I could already see myself as a Cordon Bleu chef, patronized – and eventually knighted – by admiring royalty. I would have my own chain of hotels and a different car for every day of the week. I'd be a bigger success than Clarrie ever would, nine brand-new GCSEs notwithstanding. In fact, my name would go down in history because I'd do for the omelette what Melba did for the peach . . .

Clarrie's voice broke into my musing.

"I could just fancy a mushroom omelette, kiddo," she said, "only I've gone and used up the last of the mushrooms."

"What about these, then?" asked Dad, producing a grubby paper bag. "I just bumped into our Georgie's bike (how many times have I told you not to leave it in the hall? Clarrie never does) – and they fell out of the pannier."

So that was where I'd hidden the wretched things! I felt sick. In fact, I thought I was going to faint. But I had to pull myself together because all of a sudden I felt nothing but protective love for my sister. She's not half bad when you get to know her. Murder her? Why, the very idea was ludicrous! Alarming! Downright dangerous!

"Don't touch 'em!" I yelled. "Those are poisonous toadstools! I'm collecting them for nature study. It's – er – part of a project. Like, a continual assessment thing, you know? You get five points for every deadly poisonous toadstool you find."

My dad peered into the bag, shook it up, stirred it around with his finger.

"Well, you won't get many points for these. They're mushrooms all right, every single one of 'em." (He should know; he must have gathered several tons of them in his time.) "And what that crazy teacher's thinking of . . ." he nagged on.

Oh boy! I'd flipped again! True to form, I'd proved so inattentive and dumb on Mrs Blair's nature trail that I'd stuffed my bag with genuine mushrooms after all.

"Huh!" grunted Dad disgustedly. "To think a son of mine, who lives right in the middle of the countryside, can't tell a toadstool from a mushroom! After all the times he's been out with me! I sometimes think that lad lives in a world of his own. Never listens to a thing you say. Hasn't a clue what's going on outside his thick head. He shouldn't need teachers to tell him what I've drummed into him since he was two years old – since the very first time I took him in Craydon Woods. Our Clarrie wouldn't have made such a daft mistake, I'll be bound! You only have to tell her something once, and she never forgets it."

Somebody groaned very loudly, and I think it must have been me. Suddenly I snatched the bag of mushrooms out of Dad's hand, emptied it on to the chopping board and chopped and chopped as if my life depended on hacking that board to splinters. Only, of course, that wasn't a heap of mushrooms I was reducing to friable fragments; it was my rotten, hateful sister's goody-goody heart.

Burglars!

Norman Hunter

Professor Branestawm rang the bell for his Housekeeper, and then, remembering that he'd taken the bell away to invent a new kind of one, he went out into the kitchen to find her.

"Mrs Flittersnoop," he said looking at her through his near-sighted glasses and holding the other four pairs two in each hand, "put your things on and come to the pictures with me. There is a very instructive film on this evening; all about the home life of the brussels sprout."

"Thank you kindly, sir," said Mrs Flittersnoop. "I've just got my ironing to finish, which won't take a minute, and I'll be ready." She didn't care a bent pen-nib about the brussels sprout picture, but she wanted to see the Mickey Mouse one. So while the Professor was putting on his boots and taking them off again because he had them on the wrong feet, and getting some money out of his money-box with a bit of wire, she finished off the ironing, put on her best bonnet, the blue one with the imitation strawberries on it, and off they went.

"Dear, dear," said the Professor when they got back from the pictures, "I don't remember leaving that window open, but I'm glad we did because I forgot my latchkey."

"Goodness gracious, a mussey me, oh deary deary!" cried Mrs Flittersnoop.

The room was all anyhow. The things were all nohow and it was a sight enough to make a tidy housekeeper like Mrs Flittersnoop give notice at once. But she didn't do it.

"The other rooms are the same," called the Professor from the top of the stairs. "Burglars have been."

And so they had. While the Professor and his Housekeeper had been at the pictures thieves had broken in. They'd stolen the Professor's silver teapot that his auntie gave him, and the butter-dish he was going to give his auntie, only he forgot. They'd taken the Housekeeper's picture-postcard album with the views of Brighton in it, and the Professor's best egg-cups that were never used except on Sundays.

"This is all wrong," said the Professor, coming downstairs and running in and out of the rooms and keeping on finding more things that had gone. "I won't have it. I'm going to invent a burglar catcher; that's what I'm going to invent."

"We'd better get a policeman first," said Mrs Flittersnoop.

The Professor had just picked some things up and was wondering where they went. "I'll get the policeman," he said, putting them down again and stopping wondering. So he fetched a policeman, who brought another policeman, and they both went into the kitchen and had a cup of tea while the Professor went into his inventory to invent a burglar catcher and Mrs Flittersnoop went to bed.

Next morning the Professor was still inventing. It was lucky the burglars hadn't stolen his inventory, but they couldn't do that because it was too heavy to take away, being a shed sort of workshop, big enough to get inside. They couldn't even take any of the Professor's inventing tools, because the door was fastened with a special Professor lock that didn't open with a key at all but only when you squeezed some toothpaste into it and then blew through the keyhole. And, of course, the burglars didn't know about that. They never do know about things of that sort.

"How far have you got with the burglar catcher?" asked Mrs Flittersnoop presently, coming in with breakfast, which the Professor always had in his inventory when he was inventing.

"Not very far yet," he said. In fact, he'd only got as far as nailing two pieces of wood together and starting to think what to do next. So he stopped for a bit and had his breakfast.

Then he went on inventing day and night for ever so long.

"Come and see the burglar catcher," he said one day, and they both went into his study, where a funny-looking sort of thing was all fixed up by the window.

"Bless me!" said Mrs Flittersnoop. "It looks like a mangle with a lot of arms."

"Yes," said the Professor, "it had to look like that because it was too difficult making it look like anything else. Now watch."

He brought out a bolster with his overcoat fastened round it and they went round outside the window.

"This is a dummy burglar," he explained, putting the bolster thing on the window-sill. "In he goes." He opened the window and pushed the dummy inside.

Immediately there was a lot of clicking and whirring noises and the mangle-looking thing twiddled its arms. The wheels began to go round and things began to squeak and whizz. And the window closed itself behind the dummy.

"It's working, it's working," cried the Professor, dancing with joy and treading on three geraniums in the flowerbed.

Suddenly the clicking and whizzing stopped, a trapdoor opened in the study floor and something fell through it. Then a bell rang.

"That's the alarm," said the Professor, rushing away. "It means the burglar thing's caught a burglar."

He led the way down into the cellar, and there on the cellar floor was the bolster with the overcoat on. And it was all tied up with ropes and wound round with straps and tapes so that it looked like one of those mummy things out of a museum. You could hardly see any bolster or coat at all, it was so tied up.

"Well I never," said Mrs Flittersnoop.

The Professor undid the bolster and put his overcoat on. Then he went upstairs and wound the burglar catcher up again, put on the Housekeeper's bonnet by mistake and went to the pictures again. He wanted to see the brussels sprout film once more, because he'd missed bits of it before through Mrs Flittersnoop keeping on talking to him about her sister Aggie and how she could never wash up a teacup without breaking the handle off.

Mrs Flittersnoop had finished all her housework

and done some mending and got the Professor's supper by the time the pictures were over. But the Professor didn't come in. Quite a long time afterwards he didn't come in. She wondered where he could have got to.

"Forgotten where he lives, I'll be bound," she said. "I never did see such a forgetful man. I'd better get a policeman to look for him."

But just as she was going to do that, "br-r-r-ring-ing-ing-g-g" went the Professor's burglar catcher.

"There now," cried Mrs Flittersnoop. "A burglar and all. And just when the Professor isn't here to see his machine thing catch him. Tut, tut."

She picked up the rolling-pin and ran down into the cellar. Yes, it was a burglar all right. There he lay on the cellar floor all tied up with rope and wound round with straps and tapes and things till he looked like a mummy out of a museum. And like the bolster dummy, he was so tied up you could hardly see any of him.

"Ha," cried the Housekeeper, "I'll teach you to burgle, that I will," but she didn't teach him that at all. She hit him on the head with the rolling-pin, just to make quite sure he shouldn't get away. Then she ran out and got the policeman she was going to fetch to look for the Professor. And the policeman took the burglar away in a wheelbarrow to the police station,

all tied up and hit on the head as he was. And the
burglar went very quietly. He couldn't do anything
else.

But the Professor didn't come home. Not all night
he didn't come home. But the policeman had caught
the other burglars by now and got all the Professor's
and the Housekeeper's things back, except the
postcards of Brighton, which the burglars had sent
to their friends. So they had nothing to do but look
for the Professor.

But they didn't find him. They hunted everywhere.
They looked under the seat at the pictures, but all
they found was Mrs Flittersnoop's bonnet with the
imitation strawberries on it, which they took to the

police station as evidence, if you know what that is. Anyhow they took it whether you know or not.

"Where can he be?" said the Housekeeper. "Oh! He is a careless man to go losing himself like that!"

Then when they'd hunted a lot more and still hadn't found the Professor, the Judge said it was time to try the new burglar they'd caught. So they put him in the prisoner's place in the court, and the court usher called out "'Ush" and everybody 'ushed.

"You are charged with being a burglar inside Professor Branestawm's house," said the Judge. "What do you mean by it?"

But the prisoner couldn't speak. He was too tied up and wound round to do more than wriggle.

"Ha," said the Judge, "nothing to say for yourself, and I should think not, too."

Then the policeman undid the ropes and unwound the straps and tapes and things. And there was such a lot of them that they filled the court up, and everyone was struggling about in long snaky sort of tapes and ropes and it was ever so long before they could get all sorted out again.

"Goodness gracious me!" cried Mrs Flittersnoop. "If it isn't the Professor!"

It was the Professor. There he was in the prisoner's place. It was he all the time, only nobody knew it because he was so wound up and hidden.

"What's all this?" said the Judge.

"Please, I'm Professor Branestawm," said the Professor, taking off all his five pairs of glasses, which fortunately hadn't been broken, and bowing to the court.

"Well," snapped the Judge. He was very cross because the mixed-up tangle of tapes and things had pulled his wig crooked and he felt silly. "What has that got to do with anything? Didn't you break into the Professor's house?"

"I left my key at home and got in through the window," said the Professor, "forgetting about the burglar catcher."

"That is neither here nor there," said the Judge,

"nor anywhere at all for that matter, and it wouldn't make any difference if it was. You broke into the Professor's house. You can't deny it."

"No," said the Professor, "but it was my own house."

"All the more reason why you shouldn't break into it," said the Judge. "What's the front door for?"

"I forgot the key," said the Professor.

"Don't argue," said the Judge, and he held up Mrs Flittersnoop's bonnet that the Professor had worn by mistake and left under the seat at the pictures. "This bonnet, I understand, belongs to your housekeeper."

Mrs Flittersnoop got up and bowed. "Indeed it does, your Majesty," she said, thinking that was the right way to speak to a judge, "but the Professor's welcome to it, I'm sure, if he wants it."

"There you are," said the Judge, "She says he's welcome to it if he wants it. That means she didn't give it to him, did you?"

"No," said Mrs Flittersnoop, "I thought—"

"What you thought isn't evidence," snapped the Judge.

"Well, what is evidence, then?" said Mrs Flittersnoop, beginning to get cross. "I never heard of the stuff. And I'm tired of all this talk that I don't understand. Give me my best bonnet and let me go. I've the dinner to get."

"Oh, give the woman her bonnet," said the Judge, and then he turned to the Professor.

"If it had been anybody else's house you'd broken into," he said, "we'd have put you in prison."

"Of course," said the Professor, trying on all his pairs of spectacles one after the other to see which the Judge looked best through.

"And if it had been anyone else who'd broken into your house, we'd have put him in prison," said the Judge.

"Of course," said the Professor, deciding that the Judge looked best through his blue sunglasses because he couldn't see his face so well.

"But," thundered the Judge, getting all worked up, "as it was you who broke into the house and as it was your own house you broke into, we can only sentence you to be set free, and a fine waste of good time this trial has been."

At this everyone in the court cheered, for they most of them knew the Professor and liked him and were glad everything was going to be all right. And the twelve jurymen cheered louder than anyone, although the Judge hadn't taken the least bit of notice of them and hadn't even asked them their verdict, which was very dislegal of him, if you see what I mean.

And as for Mrs Flittersnoop, she clapped her

bonnet on the Professor's head, and then several people carried him shoulder-high out of the court and home, with the imitation strawberries in Mrs Flittersnoop's hat rattling away and the Professor bowing and smiling and looking through first one pair of glasses and then another.

Barker

Peter Dickinson

There was a rich old woman called Mrs Barker who lived in a pokey little house at the top of a street so steep that it had steps instead of pavements. Mrs Barker could look all the way down the street from her windows and watch people puffing up the steps to bring her presents. Quite a lot of people did that, because Mrs Barker didn't have any sons or daughters or nieces or nephews, only what she called "sort-ofs". Sort-of-nieces, sort-of-nephews, sort-of-cousins and so on.

You want an example? Mr Cyril Blounder's mother's father's father's mother's sister had married Mrs Barker's father's mother's brother. That made Mr Blounder a very sort-of sort-of, but it didn't stop him bringing Mrs Barker lettuces from his garden and hoping that one day she'd die and leave him some money in her will. When he came Mrs Barker's maid Hannah would bring him camomile tea, which he pretended to like, while Mrs Barker looked in the lettuces for slugs.

Most of the other sort-ofs did much the same, and they always got given camomile tea, and they all pretended to like it, because of the will. When they left, Mrs Barker would stand at her window and watch them go muttering down the hill. *She* knew what they were thinking.

Whenever a new sort-of was born Mrs Barker always sent a silver napkin-ring for a christening present, with a name on it. She chose the name herself, without asking the parents, so that was what the child got called. The parents usually decided it was worth it, because of the will. Mrs Barker preferred what she called "sensible names". She wrote them down in the back of her notebook to make sure she didn't choose the same one twice.

After that Mrs Barker paid no attention to the child until it was eight years old. Then she used to send a message inviting it to tea. So the parents would dress the child in its smartest clothes and take it up the steps, reminding it several times on the way to say "Please" and "Thank you" and not to make faces when it drank the camomile tea. (Some parents used to give their children camomile tea for a week before the visit, for practice.)

But more important than any of that advice was

that when Mrs Barker asked the child what it wanted for a present it must choose something *really worth having*.

Because whatever it wanted, it got.

It was very extraordinary. Mrs Barker wasn't at all generous in other ways. She sent the most miserable mingy presents to the sort-ofs at Christmas, when they all bought her beautiful things they couldn't really afford, but just this once in their lives . . .

She would peer at each child with sharp little eyes and croak in her sour old voice, "Well, what would you like for a present?" and the child would open its eyes as wide as it could and say a racing-bike *please* or a pony *please* or a huge model railway lay-out *please* . . . Mrs Barker would write the request down in her notebook and put it away, but when the child was gone she would take out the notebook and cross off one of the names in the back.

A few days later the present would come, and it would be the best you could buy – the bike with the most gears, the briskest little pony, the most complicated railway set. But it would be the last good present that child ever got from Mrs Barker.

All this went on for years and years, until there were sort-ofs who'd been to tea with Mrs Barker when *they* were eight, now taking their own children up the steps and telling them to say please and thank you and above all to choose a present *really worth having* . . .

One of these later sort-ofs was called Molly. (Her parents had hoped to call her Claudinetta, but it said Molly on her ring.) She was taken up the steps wearing a pink bow in her hair and a pale blue frock with a white lacy apron crackling new, and told all the usual things. Hannah opened the door for her and asked the parents to be back at half-past five, and Molly went in alone.

As soon as the door was shut, Molly undid the ribbon in her hair and took off the lacy apron and put them on a chair in the hall before she went into Mrs Barker's parlour and shook hands. Mrs Barker's hand was cold and dry, with loose slithery skin. She pursed her purple lips and peered at Molly.

"You were wearing a pink bow when you came up the steps," she said.

"I took it off," said Molly.

Mrs Barker puffed out her cheeks like a frog, but didn't say anything. Hannah brought in the tea, thin little sandwiches, tiny dry cakes and a steaming teapot.

"Do you like camomile tea?" she asked.

"Not much, thank you, but I'll drink it if you want me to."

Mrs Barker puffed out her cheeks again and peered at Molly, craning her neck like an old tortoise.

"What do you drink at home?" she said.

"Milk. Or orange juice. Or just water."

Mrs Barker tinkled a small glass bell and when Hannah came in she told her to bring Molly a glass of milk. After that they ate tea. Then they played an old-fashioned card game. Then they did a jigsaw. And then Mrs Barker glanced out of the window and said, "I can see your father coming up the steps. It is time for you to go. Would you like me to put the bow back in your hair?"

Molly ran and fetched the ribbon and apron and Mrs Barker tied them with trembling old fingers.

"Now," she said, "I expect you would like a present."

Molly had been meaning to ask for a record-player, though she hadn't felt comfortable about it. Her parents had been so eager, so excited about the idea of a present *really worth having*, and now there was something strange in Mrs Barker's dry old voice, as though she was getting herself ready for a disappointment . . .

So without thinking Molly said what she'd felt all along.

"I don't think people should give each other presents till they know each other properly."

Mrs Barker puffed out her cheeks.

"Very well," she said.

"Thank you all the same," said Molly. "And thank you for the tea."

Then her father knocked on the door and took her home.

Naturally her family wanted to know what she'd chosen for a present, and when she said nothing they didn't believe her. But nothing came and nothing came and they were furious, while all the other sort-ofs were filled with glee. (None of the sort-of families liked each other much, but that didn't stop them passing the gossip round.)

Then, several weeks later, a message came that

Mrs Barker would like Molly to come to tea again, and she was not to dress up specially. This time there were hot buttered scones and fresh chocolate cake and not a whiff of camomile tea anywhere. But nothing was said about presents.

The same thing happened a few weeks later, and a few weeks later still. Now Molly's family was filled with glee and all the other sort-ofs were furious. None of their children had ever been asked to a second tea, so it was obvious Mrs Barker had decided at last who was going to get her money, and now it was too late to tell the children the trick was not to ask the old so-and-so for anything at all.

This went on till almost Christmas, when a letter came.

My dear Molly,

I believe you and I may by now be said to know each other properly, so it is time we exchanged presents. You told me on your last visit that your family dog was about to have puppies. Would you choose one for me, and I shall send you something on Christmas Day.

Yours affctntly,
Ethelswitha Barker

The family dog was a mongrel, and nobody could guess who the father of her last litter might be. Molly's parents wanted to sneak off and buy a beautiful pedigree pup and pretend it came from the litter, but Molly said Mrs Barker was much too sharp not to spot that. She chose a black-and-white male and took it up the hill to show Mrs Barker, who said Molly was to take it home and look after it till it was house-trained. She added that it was to be called Barker. (A sure sign, most of the sort-ofs thought, that she was losing her wits. Naming a dog after your dead husband – honestly!)

Molly's Christmas present turned out to be a yellow waterproof hat and coat and a pair of blue wellies – for taking Barker for walks in wet weather, the note that came with them said.

When he was house-trained Barker went to live with Mrs Barker, and Molly would go most days to take him for a walk. Sometimes she stayed for tea, sometimes not. Time passed. More sort-ofs climbed the hill for their first tea. If they asked for presents they got them, and if they didn't Mrs Barker sent a cheque and note telling the parents to buy something the child needed.

Then people noticed that the writing on the notes was getting shaky. Next they saw the doctor going up the steps to the pokey little house three times in one week. Then an ambulance came. Soon after that Mrs Barker died. All this while Molly took Barker for walks, as usual.

All the sort-ofs were invited to hear the will read. They came, grinding their teeth, except for Molly's parents who did their best not to look too triumphant, though they'd already decided on the grand house outside the town which Molly was going to buy with her money. It had a lovely big garden for her to run about in.

By the time the lawyer had finished reading the will *everybody* was grinding their teeth.

Mrs Barker had left some money to Hannah for her to retire and be comfortable. That wasn't too bad. But then she had left the rest, the whole lot, an enormous amount, to Barker!

And they weren't even going to get their hands on it when Barker died. After that it was going to charity. Until then it was all Barker's. Molly was to be Barker's guardian. There was a lot of legal language, with trustees and heaven knows what, but what it all meant was that Molly was the only person who knew what Barker wanted. If she said Barker was to have something, he was to get it. If not, the money stayed in the bank. And provided Barker lived till Molly was sixteen, she was the one who was going to choose the charities which got the money in the end.

Some of the sort-ofs talked about going to law to have the will altered, but the lawyers said it was all very carefully drawn up and in any case no one could be sure who would get the money if they did get the will changed – it would probably have gone straight to the charities. So they decided to put up with it.

Almost at once Molly's parents realized this mightn't be too bad, after all. Barker needed a big garden to run about in, didn't he, and it happened there was this suitable house outside the town . . .

Molly said she'd go and see what Barker thought (though really she spent most of the time talking to Hannah). When she came back she said Barker wanted to stay in his own home, with Hannah to look after him, and Hannah didn't mind. (It was her home too – she'd lived there since she was sixteen.)

Molly's parents were *not* pleased and there was a real row, but Molly stuck to her guns. She kept saying Barker had made up his mind. Her father stormed off to the lawyers next morning, but they said the same thing. It was absolutely clear. If Molly said Barker wanted to stay in his own house, that was that. You may think it was tough-minded of Molly to stick it out, but she was a tough-minded girl. Perhaps that was why Mrs Barker had chosen her.

And she had something to help her. On the day the will had been read one of the lawyers had given her a letter and told her she wasn't to show it to anyone else. He hadn't even read it himself. It said:

My dear Molly,

You will now know the contents of my will. It is no doubt very selfish of me to amuse myself in this manner, but I am a selfish old person and that's that. When I was young I inherited a ridiculous amount of money, but it was all tied up in Trusts until I was twenty-five, so I got no fun out of it when I was a child. I have always resented this.

I see no reason why any of my connections should inherit my money. It will do far more good if it goes to charity, but it amuses me to think that before that a child might have some fun spending a little of it, as I never did. That is why I devised a little test to choose a child who was likely to be level-headed about money. I am glad it was you who passed the test.

If I were to leave the money to you till you are of age, people would insist on it being spent "for your own good", and you would have very little say in the matter. That is why I have left it to Barker. My will says you are to be his guardian, but really it is the other way about. He is there to protect you – you are quite clever enough to see how useful he will be in his role. I strongly advise you to establish the point at the earliest possible moment.

Barker is an earnest soul (as I am not), and I think he will make a very good guardian.

Yours affctntly,
Ethelswitha Barker

So Molly did what the letter suggested and "established the point". She liked their own home, and so did her parents, really. The other one was much too grand for them, and after a few weeks her parents began to think so too.

But soon the other sort-ofs realized that Molly's family weren't the only ones who could suggest things Barker might like. They would stop Molly while she was taking him for one of his walks and say he looked a bit off-colour, and wouldn't a bit of sea-air do him good? Now it happened there was this holiday villa in Cornwall, a real snip, though he wouldn't want to use it all the time, would he, and maybe when he wasn't there it would be best if one of the Frossetts (or the McSniggs, or the Blounders, or the Globotzikoffs, or which ever of the sort-of families had thought of the scheme), went and took care of the place. For a suitable fee, perhaps.

Molly said Barker would think it over. The following week, she explained Barker thought he'd like to go on a rabbiting holiday this year, with Molly, of course, but he didn't want her to be lonely so she'd better bring a few friends and her Mum and Dad to drive him about to good rabbiting places. Barker paid for the petrol and the hotel rooms.

A bit later a new baby sort-of was born and had to be christened. Barker sent a silver napkin-ring, but without a name on it. Privately Molly wondered what would have happened if she'd told the silversmith to put "Bonzo", but she explained that Barker didn't think it was quite right for a dog to tell people what to call their children.

And then one day in the supermarket Molly heard two mothers of sort-of families chatting about the old days, and the excitement of taking their children up to have tea with Mrs Barker, and thinking of *really worthwhile* presents, and wondering whether by any chance little Sam or Betsy would be the one . . .

Molly talked to Barker about it on their next walk, and the upshot was that the notes started coming again, inviting the children to tea when it was their turn. It was a bit different, because Barker didn't ask the questions the way Mrs Barker used to, and the food was better, and there was Molly to talk to and play with, but there was always camomile tea (or that's what Molly said it was, though it didn't taste much different from ordinary tea).

In fact it all became rather like an old custom, which people have forgotten the reason for, but go on doing because they've always done it and it's a bit picturesque and so on. And there were the presents, of course. They were as good as ever, but somehow it didn't seem quite so mean and grabby asking for them, which is what most people, in their heart of hearts, had probably felt, just as Molly had. And nobody now thought that Barker was going to leave all his money to a child who said "Please" and "Thank you" properly or an adult who turned up on the doorstep with a particularly nice present.

Mr Cyril Blounder, quite early on, did climb the steps one day with a bone he swore he'd dug up in his allotment though it looked remarkably fresh. Hannah gave him camomile tea on the doorstep, and all the other sort-ofs felt he'd made a fool of himself and nobody else tried it.

Time passed. Nothing much new happened. Molly got older, and so did Barker. You'd have thought he was rather a dull dog if you met him, but he had interesting ideas. He longed to travel, Molly said, but he couldn't because of the quarantine, so instead he used to send Hannah and her sister who lived somewhere up in the North on annual holidays to exciting places, and Hannah would come back and show him her slides. He gave generously to charities on flag-days – not only to the RSPCA – and took a keen interest in nature preservation. He had some handsome trees planted in the park, with a bench under them which said:

IN FOND MEMORY OF ETHELSWITHA BARKER
Loving Mistress

Strangers didn't know quite what to make of that, but none of the local people thought it odd.

In fact, one year there was a proposal to have Barker elected Mayor. It was only half-serious, of course, but it worried the real parties enough to pay lawyers to find to whether you can elect a dog mayor, which you can't. But he might have got in. For a dull dog, he was surprisingly popular.

One lucky result from Barker's point of view was

that he got quite an active love-life. In a town like that most people had pedigree dogs and used to send the bitches off to be mated. They tried to shoo mongrels away when their bitches were on heat, but it almost became a sort of status symbol to let your bitch have one litter of Barker's pups, so after a few years there were quite a lot of his children in the town – Barker's own sort-ofs. They weren't sort-ofs because their relationship with him was complicated, like Mrs Barker's had been. He was their father and they were his children. That was usually clear from the black-and-white patches. They were sort-of collies and sort-of Labradors and sort-of dachshunds and so on.

Curiously, people didn't mind having these mongrels born to their prize bitches, and even more curiously this wasn't because Barker was so rich – he didn't send the family a huge present when it happened, only the right number of collars, with names for the puppies on them. It was because the whole town was proud of having him around. He was odd, and different, and when nothing much was happening in the world reporters would come and write stories for their newspapers about him.

Of course they never got it quite right – reporters don't. It was difficult for them to understand the difference it made, all that money belonging to a dog, and not a person. When old Mrs Barker had been alive people used to think about her money a lot, envying her or scheming how to wheedle cash out of her, or complaining about her not spending it on things they thought important. But somehow when the money belonged to a dog it stopped being so serious. There were still schemes and complaints, of course (you don't change people *that* much), but whoever was listening to the schemer or complainer was always likely to switch the conversation into jokes about Barker, almost as though the money wasn't real. It was, of course – it got trees planted and the spire repaired and it endowed nature trails and sent the over-60s on coach trips and bought a site for the Youth Club – but it didn't *matter* the way it had seemed to before. Even the sort-of families stopped being as spiteful about each other as they used to be – the money was out of everyone's reach now, so there wasn't much point.

Dogs don't live as long as humans, so it wasn't long before people started to fuss about Barker's health, and knit coats for him to wear in the winter – though he had a perfectly good thick coat of his own – and speak sharply to delivery-men who hurtled round corners in their vans. Barker was a fool about traffic. Of course Hannah was supposed to keep him locked in and Molly always fastened his lead when they were walking anywhere near roads, but if he saw a cat or smelt a rabbit there was absolutely no holding him, or he'd manage to slip out on one of his love-affairs while Hannah had the door open to take in the milk. The Town Council had notices put up at the most dangerous places, saying CAUTION: DOG CROSSING, but they weren't much use as Barker never crossed twice in the same place.

Still, he bore a charmed life for eight years. He had lots of narrow escapes. Strangers driving through sometimes hit lampposts or traffic islands trying to avoid him, and they couldn't understand why everybody was furious with *them* and why there were always a dozen witnesses ready to come forward saying it was *their* fault.

The over-60s coach got him in the end – coming back from a trip Barker had paid for himself. Molly said that Barker had always wanted a really good send-off, so there was a jolly funeral with masses to eat and drink for the whole town, and a fun-fair and fireworks.

After that Molly spent a whole week with the lawyers, organizing which charities should get Barker's money. Practically all of it went to ordinary sensible places, a bit to the RSPCA of course, but mostly things like Cancer Research and War on Want. But Molly kept one per cent aside (that doesn't sound very much, but Mrs Barker really had been enormously rich, so it was still a useful amount) for a special charity she had set up. The lawyers had had a lot of trouble making it legal, but she'd insisted it was what Barker wanted, so they managed it somehow.

That was why all the families in the town which had one of Barker's puppies as their pet got a surprise cheque through the letter box, with a letter saying it was to be spent exclusively for the benefit of their dog, and the youngest person in the house was the only one who could say what that dog wanted.

It was an idea that would have amused Mrs Barker, Molly thought and made her wrinkle her lips into her sour little smile – sort-ofs getting something in the end. Only not her sort-ofs. Barker's.

The Man with the Silver Tongue

Rory McGrath

There was no doubt about it, Herbert Cragnut was born with a silver tongue. Anyone who met him when he was a young lad said, "Herbert, you have a silver tongue!" Now Herbert didn't really understand what people meant when they said this . . . and just in case *you* don't, I'll tell you. If a person has a silver tongue it means that that person is a good talker or has a clear, sweet, melodious voice. Both these things were true of Herbert. But when he was a small boy, Herbert thought people meant that his tongue was actually made out of silver. And once when he was short of pocket money around Christmas time, he even went to a jewellers to have it valued.

"What can I do for you, little boy?" asked the wizened but friendly old jeweller.

Herbert replied, "I want some money for this," and immediately stuck his tongue out.

"How dare you! Clear off," said the wizened but no longer friendly old jeweller. Herbert explained what he meant and the old man laughed and pointed out Herbert's misunderstanding. "You have a silver tongue, my boy, it's true. A beautiful clear voice. You should be an actor or a singer. You should be on stage or even in films!"

But that was a long, long time ago. Let's come up to date . . . to a modern comprehensive school where Herbert was now a bitter and bad-tempered old English teacher . . .

"I should have been an actor or a singer, I should have been on stage or even in the films . . . and not just stuck here in this miserable school teaching you disgusting flea-ridden malodorous troglodytes! Perkins, stop sniggering or I'll excoriate you till you scream for mercy."

"What does malodorous mean, sir?" asked one of the boys.

"What does troglodyte mean, sir, and excoriate?" asked another.

"What does Perkins mean?" asked Perkins cheekily.

"Right. Consider yourselves in a state of detention after school as just punition for this outrageous insurrection," said Herbert. What Herbert hated most in the world was school children. What school children hated most in the world was Herbert . . . and, of course, sprouts.

Well, actually there was one pupil who quite liked Herbert and marvelled at his voice and his words. He was called Walker, but on account of his large sticky-out ears everyone called him "Lugs". Lugs would often stay behind and talk to Herbert about some of the long impressive-sounding words. And of course Lugs realized that Herbert was in fact a very good teacher if only he didn't lose his temper so quickly and so often. Herbert was quite flattered by

the youngster's attention and found that he didn't despise Lugs as much as the others.

But in general, though, Herbert would shout and scream insults at his pupils all day long and they would just smirk or snigger. This made him even more angry. The reason the kids sniggered, of course, was because they could never understand Herbert's insults. The silver-tongued schoolmaster used such long and complicated words that they meant nothing to the boys. He called them things like "scurrilous scrofulations", "putrescent amoebas", "coprophagous cretins" or "purulent prominences" and the boys and girls, well, they just shrugged their shoulders and laughed.

If he'd called them "spotty scumbags" or "snot-faced toe-rags" they might have shut up and had more respect for Herbert. But they had such contempt for Mr Cragnut that they didn't even bother thinking up a nickname for him. Oh, they had nicknames for the other teachers. The headmaster, for example, talked with a sizzling breathy voice and they called him "Hissing Sid". The chemistry teacher was a small man who always looked as if he'd just come out of a rainstorm, they called him "Dripdry", and there was the PE teacher who had been a policeman and who'd once had a metal plate inserted into his knee after an accident. They called him "Robocop". There were many others: "Dismal Desmond," "Humpy", "Ollie Beak", "Pizza-face Prat", but as for Herbert Cragnut, they just called him Herbert. Or more often, that great big herbert, Herbert.

Herbert was annoyed that the children had been naughty. It meant he had to give them detention, which annoyed him because that meant *he* had to stay behind as well.

That annoyed him because it meant he missed his usual bus and had to get a rush hour bus and that annoyed him because the only seat that was left was upstairs. Now that doubly annoyed Herbert, firstly because the bus always started as he was only half-way up the stairs and he invariably lost his balance and fell backwards, lunging rather unflatteringly at the rail. Secondly going upstairs meant he had to sit in the smoking section and smoking really annoyed Herbert.

"You ignorant plebs," he shouted as he sat down on the bus. "Kindly desist from your noxious exhalations. Do you not realize you are turning each molecule of our mutual atmosphere into a microscopic venomous projectile!"

"Sit down and shut up," shouted someone at the back.

An old lady whispered to her friend, "We always seem to get a nutter on the 134."

But the man next to him said, "Well said, I quite agree." But this man annoyed Herbert just as much because he had a silly moustache and a bow-tie. And Herbert hated those prissy vainglorious affectations!

He got home in a bad temper, he went to bed in a bad temper, he dreamed he was in a giant bad temper with sixteen floors and lots of windows. He woke up in a bad temper, had breakfast in a bad temper, shaved in a bad temper and had some tea in a . . . large blue and white cup.

But as he was leaving the house he noticed there was a message on the answerphone. "That's odd," he thought. "I turned the answerphone off before I went to bed." He pressed the playback button and listened. "BEEEEP I thought I'd better let you know I'm leaving you. Or rather I left you last night. I just got fed with all the bad temper and the shouting and the insults and the long words which no one understands, not even me! BEEEP!" Herbert was stunned! It was his voice on the answerphone.

"   !" said Herbert. "   !" He repeated.

Then a thought struck him. When he spoke just then nothing came out! It was just silence. And then the horror and the terror struck him. It wasn't *him* on the answerphone. It was his *voice*! His voice had left him.

He was still recovering from the shock a few hours

later when he walked into the Police Station carrying a large box full of bits of card. His embarrassment was now cancelling out the shock of what had happened.

Shaking slightly he handed a card to the station sergeant who read what was on it.

"'I've ... lost ... my ... voice!' Oh I see, sir, well don't worry, just write everything down, no problem. What can we do for you?" Herbert handed the same card back to the policeman.

"'I've lost my voice'. Ah, listen, sir. I understand. I often lose my voice myself. Just write down what you've come to the Police Station for. Are you here to report something, to ask for something, to give us some information or what?" Herbert wrote something else on the card. The sergeant read it out!

"'I've lost my voice. That's it. Some people lose their dogs, I've lost my voice!'" The officer was perplexed. "You've lost your voice like other people lose their dogs?" Herbert smiled and nodded. "So ... er ... your voice might have been run over by a car? Or it may have been stolen by a voice-lover who didn't already have a voice like yours? Or perhaps your voice got lost while chasing rabbits round the common?"

Herbert realized the policeman wasn't taking him seriously. He picked out another card from the box and handed it to the sergeant who read it out.

" 'I woke up this morning; my voice had gone. It left a message on the answerphone but it didn't say where it had gone!'" The sergeant was beginning to think that Herbert wasn't taking *him* seriously. He glanced up at the calendar to see if it was April the First. It wasn't. The sergeant was absolutely stumped; he didn't know what to do. So he resigned from the Police Force there and then and went off to live in Devon and grow tomatoes. That didn't help Herbert who was waiting at the Police Station front desk. A young bright-looking policeman walked in and Herbert handed him a card. The young constable read it.

" 'Have any voices been handed in?' Er . . . I'll go and check," he said. After a few minutes he returned with three boxes. "Is it one of these?" asked the young PC, and he opened the first box. Herbert heard a voice come out of the box.

"I'll tell you what, son, it's been a terrible week for the nags. All this rain has made swamps of the courses," said a broad Irish accent. Herbert shook his head and the constable opened the second box. "Ninety-two years old I am, ninety-two I can remember as far back as . . . er . . . when was it now . . . nineteen something it was . . . and the King, or possibly the Queen . . ." the old croaky voice trailed off. Herbert shook his head again and they tried the third box. "Allo, m'sieu. Could you please tell me the best route to the Palace of Buckingham? I would like to see the guards being changed." Another blank. Herbert went home a sad and broken man.

Herbert couldn't possibly go back to school. He had to find his voice. So he drew his curtains and put a note on the door saying "Visiting a sick aunt in Australia. Back in a few weeks." By day he'd slip out in disguise in search of his voice. But in vain. He was distraught. He began thinking that even teaching school children was better than having no voice. He thought to himself, "If ever I get my voice back, I might start being nice to those little blighters!"

Meanwhile three of Herbert's pupils were playing in Bogle Cave a few miles from the town. They were Gary, Lee and Lugs. The stalactites and stalagmites made the three children feel they were inside the mouth of a giant shark surrounded by savage teeth.

"It's like being inside the mouth of a giant shark surrounded by savage teeth!" said Lugs.

"How do you know?" challenged Gary. "Have you ever been inside the mouth of a giant shark?"

"No," said Lugs.

"Well, shut up then," answered Gary.

"Stop arguing," said Lee. "Let's get out of here, I'm frightened!"

In truth, they were all a bit frightened. Bogle Cave

73

was a weird place. The walls glistened with slime and crawled with strange insects that had eerie glowing tails. The ceiling dripped constantly with freezing water and occasionally the torch light picked out the ugly shapes of sleeping bats hanging from the roof like leather rags.

"All right then, we'll go if you're scared," said Gary who was a bit superstitious and remembered that he'd read somewhere that bats swooped down on you and sucked blood from your neck and when you woke up you were a bat as well and couldn't see yourself in the mirror or eat garlic.

"Wait a minute," said Lugs. "We can't go until we've heard the echo! All caves have an echo. We've got to shout something. Hello!" shouted Lugs.

"Hello!" came the echo loud and clear.

"Goodbye," shouted Lee who was even more frightened now.

"Goodbye," shouted back the echo very distinctly.

Lugs shouted again. "My name is Mickey Walker but everyone calls me Lugs."

The echo came back immediately.

"I know!" The children stared at each other in horror. Then they screamed and ran for it!

"Help, help, help!" they cried.

"Don't go, don't go, don't go!" echoed the echo. But they had gone.

On his way home, Lugs couldn't stop thinking about the echo. It seemed to be not just an echo but a voice in its own right . . . and a fine deep voice too . . . and a voice he recognized. The voice of Herbert Cragnut.

Herbert picked up the note that was lying on the doormat. It was written in a hand he recognized. It was Lugs' writing. "Why don't you come back to school?" the note said. "It can't be much fun hiding in Bogle Cave." Herbert, of course, hadn't been hiding in Bogle Cave at all. But he knew immediately what the note meant. His voice was hiding in Bogle Cave. He'd go there straight away and plead with his voice to come back. But how would he start a conversation with his voice without his voice? "I'll take the answerphone," he thought. "On it is a recording of me saying, 'Hello this is Herbert Cragnut.'" This was a very clever idea, he thought.

"Hello, this is Herbert Cragnut," rang out the answerphone in the dank cave.

"Hello, this is Herbert Cragnut," came the reply. Herbert tried it again a few times. Every time the echo came back the same. "Hello, this is Herbert Cragnut." Herbert knew that the echo was really his voice so he decided to just sit there and wait for his voice to make the next move . . . or the next sound. After about half an hour the echo boomed through the cave.

"All right then. You win. It is me." Herbert smiled. "I thought you'd find me eventually."

"   !" said Herbert.

"And tell me why I should come back," said Herbert's voice.

"   ," said Herbert.

"You can't live without me. Ha ha ha ha. Very funny," said Herbert's voice. "Well I can live without the constant angry shouting and insulting. I am a fine voice. I should be giving pleasure not pain!"

"   !" said Herbert.

"Of course, I'm right!" said Herbert's voice.

"   ," said Herbert.

"All right then, explain!" said Herbert's voice. So Herbert explained.

"   ." He explained how he'd set his heart on being an actor or a singer or some sort of entertainer when he was a boy but his parents said he was silly, that show business was a wicked and risky business and he should study hard and get a really sensible steady job like teaching. They were both teachers and they were comfortable and happy. Though Herbert never remembered them smiling a lot. They certainly never laughed. They wouldn't let him take part in the school plays; they wouldn't take him to the cinema or the theatre and wouldn't let him go on his own. He became an average boring teacher. He hated the children he taught. Especially the ones who had lovely voices, especially the ones who sang, especially the ones in the school play and of course the ones who chatted about the latest play or film their parents had taken them to see. His silver tongue had got tarnished. There was a nasty bitter taste in his mouth.

After hearing his tale Herbert's voice was speechless.

"I . . . I . . . just don't know what to say. I know, I'll make a deal with you," it said firmly.

"   !" said Herbert. So Herbert's voice outlined the deal and Herbert agreed. From now on

Herbert Cragnut's beautiful voice would never be used in anger or insult. It was a very happy Herbert who sat on the top deck of the bus back into town. He and his voice were chatting amiably.

"It's really nice having you back. Well I'm looking forward to a happy partnership. So am I. I did miss you, you know. I bet you did."

The old woman in the seat behind turned to her friend and said, "We always seem to get a nutter on the 134."

Herbert didn't go back to teaching. He decided to do what he always wanted to do: become an entertainer and use his voice to the best of his ability. And in a short time he became one of the most popular entertainers in the country. Amusing for adults and delightful for children. Herbert Cragnut had become a ventriloquist. He had his dummy made especially with sticky-out ears and called him Lugs in honour of the boy who'd helped him to find his voice. And when you saw him do his act with Lugs on his knee you'd swear that the voice was coming from the dummy, which spoke in a melodious, distinct, rich, fruity voice, while Herbert sat there not moving his lips at all. Sometimes he'd drink a glass of water and the dummy would still be talking . . . sometimes he'd leave the stage altogether and the dummy would still be talking.

"Sorry about him," said the dummy. "He has to go home, it's way past his bedtime. I'll finish the show without him!" It was sensational. The audience was astounded. Herbert got into the finals of a national talent competition and out of two hundred entrants came a staggering second. Herbert didn't mind coming second. He actually preferred the runners-up medal which was, of course, silver!

Double Bluff

Helen Cresswell

"There is no point in your telling me Anthea has turned into a penguin," his mother said. "You've already tried that half a dozen times this morning, and I've told you – I don't believe it. Where is Anthea, anyway?"

"In the bathroom," said Timothy. "I've run some cold water into the bath. I thought it would make her feel more at home."

"I see. Would you like some ice cubes? You could float those in the bath and make-believe it was Greenland."

"Good idea."

He went to the fridge.

"Blow!" he said. "Only orange flavour."

He hesitated. Would these comfort Anthea if he were to drop them in the bath, or would she perhaps think he was trying to be funny?

"I'll leave it, I think," he decided. He chipped off a

couple of cubes and popped one into each cheek.

"For someone whose sister has just been translated into a penguin," said his mother, "you're taking it very coolly. Could you just move out of the kitchen? I'm trying to make a pie."

"Is it a fish pie?"

"No, it's not. Why?"

"I was thinking of Anthea. They like fishes, all right, penguins. But I'm not sure about the pie bit."

"This is chicken and ham. And I daresay she'll manage it when the time comes."

"No." He shook his head. "She won't, you know. There's no pigs in the Antarctic, and no chickens. Definitely. We've done it in geography."

"Perhaps," suggested his mother, "you might like to nip out for some whale meat?"

"I know you think I'm making it up," he said. "I told you   come and look for yourself."

"And I told you – I don't mind playing games if I can get on with the lunch at the same time. If only it would stop raining and you could get outside."

"Poor old Anthea," said Timothy. "I'll go back up, anyway. Somebody ought to cheer her up."

"Doesn't she like being a penguin, then?"

"She hates it. She says the minute she gets turned back she's going to give me a real thumping. She's already had a go at me, with her flippers."

"It was your fault then, was it?"

"We-ell . . ." He considered the question. "It was yours, in a kind of way. It was you who gave me that magic set for Christmas. And with all the instructions being in Chinese, how did *I* know what would happen?"

"I thought it would be fun for you to try it out for yourself," she said. "See what happened."

"I did. And something did happen. Anthea turned into a penguin. I'm going back up."

The penguin was standing in the bath flipping her feet disconsolately and sending up a spray that was landing on the floor, mostly.

"You do like it in there, then?" said Timothy.

"Like it?" shrilled the penguin. "I hate it! I'm only here so's I can get everything soaked and then you'll catch it. What did Mother say?"

"She didn't believe me. Kept making jokes about it."

"Jokes?" The penguin threshed furiously. "Isn't she even coming up?"

"Wouldn't. She's making a ham and chicken pie. It smells ace."

"What I'd like," said the penguin – not exactly between clenched teeth, more between gritted beak – "would be to turn you into a chicken and ham pie, and eat you!"

"Couldn't," he told her. "Not either. Penguins don't eat ham and chicken pies."

"This one would," said Anthea Cunningham, who had only an hour previously been a ten-year-old with long fair hair and blue eyes and was now a penguin, and might be for the rest of her life, for all she knew.

"I'm sorry," said Timothy. "I really am beginning to feel sorry for you."

"Thank you very much," said the penguin, with a swift swipe of a flipper that caught him wetly behind the ear. He ducked back.

"If you're going to be like that," he said, "I shan't even try to help. And it was as much your fault as mine – you can't read Chinese any more than I can. And you're older than me. If you'd been able to read Chinese this would never have happened."

"You'll be saying next," said the penguin, "that if I hadn't been born in the first place this would never have happened!"

Timothy thought for a moment.

"Well, it wouldn't, would it? Come to think of it."

His words were greeted with the wettest yet spray of cold water.

"The only thing I can think of," he said, "is to try something else out of the box. See what happens. If there's a spell for turning people into penguins, there ought to be one for turning them back again. Else people would want their money back."

"That's true," she agreed. "That's the first sensible remark you've made today."

"I'll get it."

Timothy laid the large box as far as possible from the spray area. He did not want water in his spells.

"The trouble is . . . what? I mean, it could be any of these."

"Try the one next to it," suggested Anthea.

"It's a bit of a bright colour," said Timothy dubiously.

"All the more likely to work. Go on. Do it. Sprinkle some over me, like you did with the other stuff."

"But what if it turned you *into* that colour?"

"Oh, don't be stupid!" snapped the penguin. Whoever heard of a pink penguin? Go on, do it!"

"Promise not to splash while I'm doing it?"

"Promise."

Timothy advanced towards the bath, then unstoppered the phial of pink powder and held it poised. Just before sprinkling it, he did what he had been longing to do all morning – he actually touched the penguin's silky head.

"Gosh!" he thought. "It *is* a penguin – actually!"

He sprinkled a little shower of the pink dust over the dark head, shut his eyes, tapped three times with the little ivory wand and said a spell three times very quickly. Then he took a step backwards and opened his eyes. He yelped and leapt back again.

The penguin was a bright flamingo pink. Only its little gold eyes remained unchanged.

"Oh, *now* we've done it!"

It seemed to Timothy that while his parents might have become reconciled in time to the idea of a penguin in the family, they were going to draw the line at this foreign-looking, rather stout bird in shocking pink.

"You – wait!" the words came out as a hiss and he backed away again and trod on the magic box.

"I'm sorry – I really am! You look *awful* now –

horrible! But it was you that made me do it."

The penguin began to cry.

"You've ruined my whole l-life!" it sobbed. "Now what will happen to me? At least before I could have gone and lived in a zoo, and had an ordinary sort of life! But now I'm a f-f-freak!"

"You certainly are," agreed Timothy fervently. "I honestly have never seen such a horrible sight in my life."

"Ooooh!" The pink penguin's wail went high and desperate.

"I think Mother *had* better come up."

He went back downstairs. He sniffed appreciatively as he entered the kitchen.

"*That* smells good!" and he felt sorrier than ever for his pink sister.

"How's the penguin?" asked his mother.

"That's what I've come about. It's got worse than ever now. She's gone a horrible bright pink – you know, sort of fluorescent, like you see on posters."

"Pink *and* a penguin?" she enquired. "Or just pink?"

"Both. She's crying now, and I don't blame her. I think you ought to go up and comfort her."

"If I go upstairs and find a bright pink penguin in my bathroom," she said, "I'm more likely to faint than start comforting."

"It's certainly enough to make anyone faint. But in a way, she's lucky. I mean, for instance, she'll never have to go to school again. Or practise the piano. I think once she gets used to the idea, she'll see the advantages."

"Would you just go up and tell her," said his mother, "that I'm dishing up in five minutes?"

"Gosh!" came a voice behind them. "That smells gorgeous!"

Timothy turned. Anthea smiled at him.

"You – you've turned back!" he said accusingly.

"I've – what?"

"Changed back."

"What from?"

"From a pink penguin, of course!"

"Pink penguin? What *are* you talking about?"

"It's a game he's been having, dear," said their mother. "I've been getting bulletins on you all morning. Last time I heard you were a phosphorescent pink penguin in floods of tears."

"Honestly!" Anthea put on her superior face. "You do think of the most ridiculous games!"

"If you can't remember," said Timothy stubbornly, "then all I can say is, that the spell must have made you lose your memory, as well. Yes, I expect that's it. You wait till you get your next test at school. You won't be able to remember a thing."

"Idiot!" She turned away.

Timothy turned to his mother.

"Look," he said, "who do you believe? Her or me?"

She hesitated.

"We'll put it this way," she said. "As soon as we've had lunch and washed up, if it's still raining and you can't go out, I'll let you try a spell on me. How would that do?"

A slow smile spread over his face.

"Oh, that will be very good," he said. "Very good indeed."

And with that he went into a corner and began to sing, under his breath, an African rain chant that had never let him down yet . . .

Jekyll and Jane

Terrance Dicks

You know that old story about Dr Jekyll and Mr Hyde?

I've never actually read the book but I saw the film on telly. It's all about this kindly old Dr Jekyll who invents some kind of magic potion. Every time he takes it he turns into horrible Mr Hyde, and goes raving round the town doing horrible deeds.

Well, we've got a Jekyll and Hyde dog. Her name's Jane. She's a mongrel with a bit of beagle in her, a smallish black and brown animal with big floppy ears, and an amazing amount of energy. The one thing she really loves is her daily walk. Luckily we live very near the Common.

It was the walks that caused all the trouble.

When we'd finally persuaded Mum and Dad to let us have a dog we'd promised to take it for a walk every weekday after school.

But you know how it is when you stagger home

from a hard day's school. All you fancy is a jam butty and a slump in front of the telly. A nice healthy walk is the last thing on your mind.

Sally and I started taking turns. Then one of us would say, "You take her today and I'll take her the next two times."

A complicated system of dog walk debts grew up and we often lost track of whose turn it really was, each insisting it was the other's go. One day we both refused to give in – and Jane didn't get her walk.

Next day at walk time Jane was nowhere in sight. She'd been out in the garden – but she wasn't there now.

Sally and I panicked and dashed out to search the Common. We looked everywhere, running up to every black and brown dog in sight, but none of them were Jane.

We staggered back home exhausted – and found Jane waiting for us on the doorstep. We made a big fuss of her, and took her inside, promising we'd never let her miss her walk again.

And we didn't – for a time. Then we got lazy again, and Jane missed another walk.

Once again she disappeared. But this time I didn't panic. "Look, she knows her way home," I said. "She'll come back when she's ready."

Sure enough, about an hour later there came a

barking at the front door. Jane was back.

"What we've got here is a self-walking dog," I said. "We might as well leave things to her."

So that's what we did. At weekends the whole family took her for long walks. On weekdays Jane made her own arrangements, leaving us free to be couch potatoes. This went on so long that we took it for granted – though somehow we never got round to telling Mum and Dad.

One day Sally read something out from the local paper. *Mystery Dog Terrorizes Common*. Apparently a number of dog walkers had complained that a huge savage dog had appeared out of nowhere and set about their beloved pets.

"I was just taking my sheepdog Bertie for a walk," said one lady. "A giant dog leaped out of the bushes barking and growling. It was brown and black with big ears and glowing eyes." Apparently she'd managed to drive the beast off with her umbrella.

Sally and I looked at each other – and at Jane who had just come back from her solo walk.

"It couldn't be . . ." said Sally.

"No, of course not," I said. "Jane's black and brown, but she's little and cute, not huge and savage. And she never gets into fights. It must be some stray dog that's gone wild. They'll catch it soon."

But they didn't. The stories went on appearing,

week after week and the mystery dog got bigger and fiercer with every story. It got into the national press and there was even a jokey item on at the end of the TV news. *Hound of the Baskervilles Returns*. Mum and Dad watched it, and they both looked at Jane.

"You'd better be careful when you're out on the Common with Jane," said Mum. "You haven't seen this monster, have you?"

"Not a sign," I said. "I think they must be making it all up." But they weren't.

One day Jane was late coming back from her walk. It was getting near the time Mum and Dad got home, and I was a bit worried. I went outside and stood on the front steps, looking down the road towards the Common wondering if I ought to go out and start searching. Suddenly I saw Jane trotting up the road towards me. I felt really relieved – but not for long.

We'd got a new neighbour next door but one, a large posh lady with a large posh poodle – one of those really big woolly ones. Its name was Fifi, it had one of those special poodle-parlour haircuts and it was her pride and joy.

As Jane came up the street the poodle and its owner came out of their house and started down the street towards her.

Suddenly Jane spotted Fifi – and the transformation began. All Jane's hair stood on end so that she really did look twice her usual size. Her lips drew back and she gave the sort of blood-curdling growl that you expect from a Doberman on a bad day. She streaked towards the poodle so fast that her ears flattened back in the slipstream.

I hurtled down the steps to intercept her. Our neighbour had stopped to chat with someone and was unaware of the monster speeding towards them. Just as Jane reached her target I grabbed her by the collar and yanked her back. I was nearly in time – but not quite. As I hauled Jane away she had a clump of woolly poodle-fur between her teeth.

There was a terrible fuss after that. Jane was growling, Fifi was howling and her owner was screaming at me.

I gave Jane a good shake and yelled, "Stop it!" You could actually see sanity return. Her fur flattened, and her head, tail and ears dropped down.

"Is that dog yours?" snapped Fifi's owner.

I was tempted to deny it – but at that moment Jane pulled away from me and dashed up the steps and into our house.

"I should like to see your parents," said the lady grimly.

"They're out," I said, and bolted up the steps after Jane. Back in the house I told Sally what had happened.

"Oh no!" she gasped. "Jane, how could you?"

Jane curled up in her basket and pretended to be asleep.

I still say what happened next wasn't really my fault. It was just bad luck. Mum came home, and I was just bracing myself to tell her the bad news when Dad got back as well, a few minutes after her as usual. He was just hanging up his coat when the doorbell rang. Jane ran to the front door and started barking.

"Good old Jane, what a watchdog," said Dad, and went to open the front door.

"Dad, wait!" I yelled, but it was too late.

Now it was fair enough Fifi's owner coming to complain. But I still say it was silly of her to bring Fifi . . .

Dad opened the door, Jane at his heels – and Jane saw Fifi standing right on her doorstep!

It was the full Jekyll and Hyde all over again. Jane's fur swelled up, her lips drew back, she gave a blood-curdling growl and she hurled herself on poor Fifi. Dad made a frantic grab at Jane's collar and pulled her back – with another chunk of poodle fur between her teeth!

Fifi's owner went into a state of total hysteria.

I must say Dad coped surprisingly well. He yelled at Jane so loudly she dived straight into her basket and didn't move for another hour. He and Mum talked themselves hoarse calming down our new neighbour, swearing that Jane must have had a touch of temporary insanity, and that she would never again be allowed anywhere near Fifi. They sympathized with Fifi's shattered nerves and promised to pay for a complete new hairdo at the poodle beauty parlour.

When they'd finally got rid of Fifi and her owner they came back into the kitchen and Mum said, "Well?"

Sally and I made a full confession. When we'd finished Dad said, "Right. Come on, you two!"

He stomped out to the car and Sally and I followed. I wasn't sure if we were being driven to the police station or the orphanage, but it turned out to be the local DIY centre.

We loaded up with wire and trellis-work, drove back home, and we all helped Dad transform the back garden into a fair imitation of a maximum security prison.

"And you two had better see she doesn't get out the front way," said Mum. "We got off lightly this time!"

Jane's days of solitary freedom are over now. She gets plenty of walks but all with human company. We keep an eye out for other dogs as well. If it's a little dog, there's nothing to worry about. If it's a smooth-coated dog of any shape or size, everything's fine.

But if the approaching dog is both large and woolly, we grab Jane quick and put her back on her lead. As we drag her past, the hair on her neck rises, just a bit, and we hear a low rumbling growl. Somewhere inside our lovable family pet, the Monster of the Common is lurking still.

These days we don't take any chances . . .

William's Busy Day

Richmal Crompton

William and the Outlaws strode along the road engaged in a lusty but inharmonious outburst of Community singing. It was the first real day of spring. The buds were bursting, the birds were singing (more harmoniously than the Outlaws) and there was a fresh invigorating breeze. The Outlaws were going fishing. They held over their shoulders their home-made rods and they carried jam jars with string handles. They were going to fish the stream in the valley. The jam jars were to receive the minnows and other small water creatures which they might catch; but the Outlaws, despite all the lessons of experience, were still hopeful of catching one day a trout or even a salmon in the stream. They were quite certain, though they had never seen any, that mighty water beasts haunted the place.

"Under the big stones," said William, "why, I bet there's all sorts of things. There's room for great big fish right under the stones."

"Well, once we turned 'em over an' there weren't any," Douglas the literal reminded him.

William's faith, however, was not to be lightly shaken.

"Oh, they sort of dart about," he explained vaguely, "by the time you've turned up one stone to see if they're there they've darted off to the next an' when you turn over the next they've darted back to the first without you seein' 'em, but they're there all the time really. I bet they are. An' I bet I catch a great big whopper – a salmon or something – this afternoon."

"Huh!" said Ginger, "I'll give you sixpence if you catch a salmon."

"A' right," said William hopefully, "an' don't you forget. Don't start pretendin' you said tuppence same as you did about me seein' the water rat."

This started a heated argument which lasted till they reached what was known locally as the cave.

The cave lay just outside the village and was believed by some people to be natural and by others to be part of old excavations.

The Outlaws believed it to be the present haunt of smugglers. They believed that smugglers held nightly meetings there. The fact of its distance from the sea did not shake their faith in this theory. As

William said, "I bet they have their meetin's here 'cause folk won't suspect 'em of bein' here. Folks keep on the lookout for 'em by the sea an' they trick 'em by comin' out here an' havin' their meetin's here where nobody's on the lookout for 'em."

For the hundredth time they explored the cave, hoping to find some proofs of the smugglers' visits in the shape of a forgotten bottle of rum or one of the lurid handkerchiefs which they knew to be the correct smuggler's headgear, or even a piece of paper containing a note of the smugglers' latest exploit or a map of the district. For the hundredth time they searched in vain and ended up gazing up at a small slit in the rock just above their heads. They had noticed it before but had not given it serious consideration. Now William gazed at it frowningly and said, "I bet I could get through that and I bet that it leads down a passage an' that," his imagination as ever running away with him, "an' that at the end of a passage there's a big place where they hold their meetin's an' I bet they're there now – *all* of 'em – holdin' a meetin'."

He stood on tiptoe and put his ear to the aperture. "Yes," he said, "I b'lieve I can hear 'em talkin'."

"Oh, come on," said Douglas, who was not of an imaginative turn of mind. "I want to catch some minnows an' I bet there aren't any smugglers there, anyway."

William was annoyed by this interruption, but, arguing strenuously, proving the presence of smugglers in the cave to his own entire satisfaction, he led his band out of the cave and on to the high road again.

The subject of smugglers soon languished. They were passing a large barrack-like house which had been in the process of building for the best part of a year. It was finished at last. Curtains now hung at the windows and there were signs of habitation – a line of clothes flapping in the breeze in the back garden and the fleeting glimpse of a woman at one of the windows. A very high wall surrounded the garden.

"Wonder what it is," said Henry speculatively, "looks to me like a prison."

"P'raps it's a lunatic asylum," said Ginger, "why's it got a high wall round it like that if it's not a lunatic asylum?"

Discussing the matter animatedly they wandered on to the stream.

"Now catch your salmon," challenged Ginger.

"All right. I bet I will," said William doggedly.

For a short time they fished in silence.

Then William gave a cry of triumph. His hook had caught something beneath one of the big stones.

"There!" he said, "I've got one. I *told* you so."

"Bet it's not a salmon," said Ginger but with a certain excitement in his voice.

"I bet it is," said William, "if it's not a salmon I – I—" with a sudden burst of inspiration, "I'll go through that hole in the cave – so there!"

He tugged harder.

His "catch" came out.

It was an old boot.

They escorted him back to the cave. The hole looked far too small for one of William's solid bulk. They stood below and stared at it speculatively.

"You've *got* to," said Ginger, "you said you would."

"Oh, all right," said William with a swagger which was far from expressing his real feelings, "I bet I can easy get through that little hole an' I bet I'll find a big place full of smugglers or smuggled stuff inside. Give me a shove . . . that's it . . . *Oo*," irritably, "don't shove so *hard* . . . You nearly pushed my head off my neck . . . Go on – go on . . . Oh, I say, I'm getting through quite easy . . . it's all dark . . . it's a sort of passage . . ." William had miraculously scraped himself through the small aperture. Two large boots was all of him which was now visible to the Outlaws. Those, too, disappeared, as William began to crawl down the passage. It was mercifully a little wider after the actual opening. His voice reached them faintly.

"It's all dark ... it's like a little tunnel ... I'm going right to the end to see what's there ... well, anyway if that wasn't a salmon I bet there *are* salmons there and I bet I'll catch one too one of these days, and—"His voice died away in the distance. They waited rather anxiously. They heard nothing and saw nothing more. William seemed to have been completely swallowed up by the rock.

William slowly and painfully (for the aperture was so small that occasionally it grazed his back and head) travelled along what was little more than a fissure in the rock. The spirit of adventure was high in him. He was longing to come upon a cave full of swarthy men with coloured handkerchiefs tied round their heads and gold earrings, quaffing goblets of smuggled rum or unloading bales of smuggled silk. Occasionally he stopped and listened for the sound of deep-throated oaths or whispers or smugglers' songs. Once or twice he was almost sure he heard them.

He crawled on and on and on and into a curtain of undergrowth and out into a field. He stopped and looked around him. He was in the field behind the cave. The curtain of undergrowth completely concealed the little hole from which he had emerged. He was partly relieved and partly disappointed. It was rather nice to be out in the open air again (the tunnel had a very earthy taste); on the other hand he had hoped for more adventures than it had afforded. But he consoled himself by telling himself that they might still exist. He'd explore that passage more thoroughly some other time – there might be a passage opening off it leading to the smugglers' cave – and meantime it had given him quite a satisfactory thrill. He'd never really thought he could get through that little hole. And it had given him a secret. The knowledge that that little tunnel led out into the field was very thrilling.

He looked around him again. Within a few yards from him was the wall surrounding the house about which they had just been making surmises. Was it a prison, or an asylum or – possibly – a Bolshevist headquarters? William looked at it curiously. He longed to know. He noticed a small door in the wall standing open. He went up to it and peeped inside. It gave on to a paved yard which was empty. The temptation was too strong for William. Very cautiously he entered. Still he couldn't see anyone about. A door – a kitchen door apparently – stood open. Still very cautiously William approached. He decided to say that he'd lost his way should anyone accost him. He was dimly aware that his appearance after his passage through the bowels of the earth was not such as to inspire confidence. Yet his curiosity and the suggestion of adventure which their surmises had thrown over the house was an irresistible magnet. Within the open door was a kitchen where a boy, about William's size and height and not unlike William, stood at a table wearing blue overalls and polishing silver.

They stared at each other. Then William said, "Hello."

The boy was evidently ready to be friendly. He replied "Hello."

Again they stared at each other in silence. This time it was the boy who broke the silence.

"What've you come for?" he said in a tone of weary

boredom. "You the butcher's boy or the baker's boy or somethin'? Only came in this mornin' so I don' know who's what yet. P'raps you're the milk boy?"

"No, I'm not," said William.

"Beggin'?" said the boy.

"No," said William.

But the boy's tone was friendly so William cautiously entered the kitchen and began to watch him. The boy was cleaning silver with a paste which he made by the highly interesting process of spitting into a powder. William watched, absorbed. He longed to assist.

"You live here?" he said ingratiatingly to the boy.

"Naw," said the boy laconically. "House-boy. Only came today," and added dispassionately, "Rotten place."

"Is it a prison?" said William with interest.

The boy seemed to resent the question.

"Prison yourself," he said with spirit.

"A lunatic asylum, then?" said William.

This seemed to sting the boy yet further.

"Garn," he said pugnaciously. "Oo're yer callin' a lunatic asylum?"

"I din' mean *you*," said William pacifically. "P'raps it's a place where they make plots."

The boy relapsed into boredom. "I dunno what they make," he said. "Only came this mornin'. *They've* gorn off to 'is *aunt* but the other one – *she's* still here, you bet, a-ringin' an' a-ringin' an' a-ringin' at her bell, an' givin' no one no peace nowheres." He warmed to his theme. "I wouldn've come if I'd knowed. Housemaid went off yesterday wivout notice. *She'd* 'ad as much as she wanted an' only the ole cook – well *I'm* not used to places wiv only a ole cook 'sides myself an' *her* upstairs a-ringin' an' a-ringin' at her bell an' givin' no one no peace nowheres an' the other two off to their aunt's. No place fit to call a place *I* don't call it." He spat viciously into his powder. "Yus, an' anyone can have my job."

"Can I?" said William eagerly.

During the last few minutes a longing to make paste by spitting into a powder and then to clean silver with it had grown in William's soul till it was a consuming passion.

The boy looked at him in surprise and suspicion, not sure whether the question was intended as an insult.

"What *you* doin' an' where *you* come from?" he demanded aggressively.

"Been fishin'," said William, "an' I jolly nearly caught a salmon."

The boy looked out of the window. It was still the first real day of spring.

"Crumbs!" he said enviously, "*fishin'*." He gazed

with distaste at his work, "an' me muckin' about with this 'ere."

"Well," suggested William simply, "you go out an' fish an' I'll go on muckin' about with that."

The boy stared at him again first in pure amazement and finally with speculation.

"Yus," he said at last, "an' you pinch my screw. Not *much!*"

"No, I won't," said William with great emphasis. "I won't. Honest I won't. I'll give it you. I don't want it. I only want," again he gazed enviously at the boy's engaging pastime, "I only want to clean silver same as you're doin'."

"Then there's the car to clean with the 'ose-pipe."

William's eyes gleamed.

"I bet I can do that," he said, "an' what after that?"

"Dunno," said the boy, "that's all they told me. The ole cook'll tell you what to do next. I specks," optimistically, "she won't notice you not bein' me with me only comin' this mornin' an' her run off her feet what with *her* ringin' her bell all the time an' givin' no one no peace an' *them* bein' away. Anyway," he ended defiantly, "I don't care if she does. It ain't the sort of place *I've* bin used to an' for two pins I'd tell 'em so."

He took a length of string from his pocket, a pin from a pincushion which hung by the fireplace, a jam jar from a cupboard, then looked uncertainly at William.

"I c'n find a stick down there by the stream," he said, "an' I won't stay long. I bet I'll be back before that ole cook comes down from *her* an' – well, you put these here on an' try'n look like me an' – I won't be long."

He slipped off his overalls and disappeared into the sunshine. William heard him run across the paved yard and close the door cautiously behind him. Then evidently he felt safe. There came the sound of his whistling as he ran across the field.

William put on the overalls and gave himself up to his enthralling task. It was every bit as thrilling as he'd thought it would be. He spat and mixed and rubbed and spat and mixed and rubbed in blissful absorption. He got the powder all over his face and hair and hands and overalls. Then he heard the sound of someone coming downstairs. He bent his head low over his work. Out of the corner of his eye he saw a large hot-looking woman enter, wearing an apron and a print dress.

"Gosh!" she exclaimed as though in despair. "Gosh! Of all the *places!*"

At that minute a bell rang loudly and with a groan she turned and went from the room again. William went on with his task of cleaning the silver. The novelty of the process was wearing off and he was beginning to feel rather tired of it. He amused himself by tracing patterns upon the surface of the silver with the paste he had manufactured. He took a lot of trouble making a funny face upon the teapot which fortunately had a plain surface.

Then the large woman came down again. She entered the kitchen groaning and saying "Oh, Lor!" and she was summoned upstairs again at once by an imperious peal of the bell. After a few minutes she came down again, still groaning and saying, "Oh, Lor! . . . First she wants hot milk an' then she wants cold milk an' then she wants beef tea an' then the Lord only knows what she wants . . . first one thing an' then another . . . I've fair had enough of it an' *them* goin' off to their aunt's an' that Ellen 'oppin' it an' *you* not much help to a body, are you?" she asked sarcastically. Then she looked at his face and screamed. "My Gosh! . . . What's 'appened to you?"

"Me?" said William blankly.

"Yes. Your face 'as gone an' changed since jus' a few minutes ago. What's 'appened to it?"

"Nothin'," said William.

"Well, it's my nerves, then," she said shrilly. "I'm startin' seein' things wrong. An' no wonder . . . Well, I've 'ad enough of it, I 'ave, an' I'm goin' 'ome . . . *now* . . . first that Ellen 'oppin' it an' then *them* goin' off

an' then 'er badgerin' the life out of me. An' then your
face changin' before me very eyes. Me nervous
system's wore out, that's what it is, an' I've 'ad
enough of it. When people's faces start changin'
under me very eyes it shows I needs a change an' I'm
goin' to 'ave one. That Ellen ain't the only one what
can 'op it. 'Er an' 'er bell-ringing – an' – an' *you* an'
your face-changin'! 'Taint no place for a respectable
woman. *You* can 'ave a taste of waitin' on 'er an' you
can tell *them* I've gone an' why – you an' your face!"

During this tirade she had divested herself of her
apron and clothed herself in her coat and hat. She
stood now and looked at William for a minute in
scornful silence. Then her glance wandered to his
operations.

"Ugh!" she said in disgust, "you nasty little
messer, you! Call yourself a house-boy – changin'
your face every minute. What d'you think you are? A
blinkin' cornelian? An' messin' about like that.
What d'you think you're doin'? Distemperin' the
silver or cleanin' it?"

At this moment came another irascible peal at the
bell.

"Listen!" said the fat woman. "'Ark at 'er! Well,
I'm orf. I'm fair finished, I am. An' you can go or stay
has you please! Serve 'em right to come 'ome an' find
us *hall* gone. Serve 'er right if you went up to 'er an'

111

did a bit of face changin' at 'er just to scare 'er same as you did me. Do 'er good. Drat 'er – an' all of you."

She went out of the kitchen and slammed the back door. Then she went out of the paved yard and slammed the door. Then she went across the field and out of the field into the road and slammed the gate.

William stood beneath the bell-dial and watched the blue disc waggle about with dispassionate interest. The little blue disc was labelled "Miss Pilliter". Then he bethought himself of his next duty. It was cleaning the car with the hose. His spirits rose at the prospect.

The bell was still ringing wildly, furiously, hysterically, but its ringing did not trouble William. He went out into the yard to find the car. It was in the garage and just near it was a hose pipe.

William, much thrilled by this discovery, began to experiment with the hose pipe. He found a tap by which it could be turned off and on, by which it could be made to play fiercely or languidly. William experimented with this for some time. It was even more fascinating than the silver cleaning. There was a small leak near the nozzle which formed a little fountain. William cleaned the car by playing on to it wildly and at random, making enthralling water snakes and serpents by writhing the pipe to and fro. He deluged the car for about a quarter of an hour in a state of pure ecstasy.

The bell could still be heard ringing in the house, but William heeded it not. He was engrossed heart and mind and soul in his manipulation of the hose pipe. At the end of the quarter of the hour he laid down the pipe and went to examine the car. He had performed his task rather too thoroughly. Not only was the car dripping outside; it was also dripping inside. There were pools of water on the floor at the back and in the front. There were pools on all the seats. Too late William realized that he should have tempered thoroughness with discretion. Still, he thought optimistically, it would dry in time. His gaze wandered round. It might be a good plan to clean the walls of the garage while he was about it. They looked pretty dirty.

He turned the hose on to them. That was almost more fascinating than cleaning the car. The water bounced back at you from the wall unexpectedly and delightfully. He could sluice it round and round the wall in patterns. He could make a mammoth fountain of it by pointing it straight at the ceiling. After some minutes of this enthralling occupation he turned his attention to the tap which regulated the flow and began to experiment with that. Laying the hose pipe flat on the floor he turned the tap in one direction till the flow was a mere trickle, then turned it in the other till it was a torrent. The torrent was more thrilling than the trickle but it was also more unmanageable. So he tried to turn the tap down again and found that he couldn't. It had stuck. He wrestled with it, but in vain. The torrent continued to discharge itself with unabated violence.

William was slightly dismayed by the discovery. He looked round for a hammer or some other implement to apply to the recalcitrant tape, but saw none. He decided to go back to the kitchen and look for one there. He dripped his way across to the kitchen and there looked about him. The bell was still ringing violently. The blue disc was still wobbling hysterically. It occurred to William suddenly that as sole staff of the house it was perhaps his duty to answer the bell. So he dripped his way upstairs. The blue disc had been marked 6. Outside the door marked six he stopped a minute, then opened the door and entered. A woman wearing an expression of suffering and a very purple dress lay moaning on the sofa. The continued ringing of the bell was explained by a large book which she had propped up against it in such a way as to keep the button pressed.

She opened her eyes and looked balefully at William.

"I've been ringing that bell," she said viciously, "for a whole hour without anyone coming to answer

114

it. I've had three separate fits of hysterics. I feel so ill that I can't speak. I shall claim damages from Dr Morlan. Never, *never* NEVER have I been treated like this before. Here I come – a quivering victim of nerves, *riddled* by neurasthenia – come here to be nursed back to health and strength by Dr Morlan, and first of all off he goes to some aunt or other, then off goes the housemaid. And I shall report that cook to Dr Morlan the minute he returns, the *minute* he returns. I'll sue her for damages. I'll sue the whole lot of you for damages; I'm going to have hysterics again."

She had them, and William watched with calm interest and enjoyment. It was even more diverting than the silver cleaning and the hose pipe. When she'd finished she sat up and wiped her eyes.

"Why don't you *do* something?" she said irritably to William.

"All right – what?" said William obligingly, but rather sorry that the entertainment had come to an end.

"Fetch the cook," snapped the lady, "ask her how she *dare* ignore my bell for hours and *hours* and HOURS. Tell her I'm going to sue her for damages. Tell her—"

"She's gone," said William.

"*Gone!*" screamed the lady. "Gone where?"

"Gone off," said William; "she said she was fair finished an' went off."

"When's she coming back? I'm in a most critical state of health. All this neglect and confusion will be the *death* of my nervous system. When's she coming back?"

"Never," said William. "She's gone off for good. She said *her* nervous system was wore out an' went off – for good."

"Her nervous system indeed," said the lady, stung by the cook's presumption in having a nervous system. "What's anyone's nervous system compared with mine? Who's in charge of the staff, then?"

"Me," said William simply. "I'm all there is left of it."

He was rewarded by an even finer display of hysterics than the one before. He sat and watched this one, too, with critical enjoyment as one might watch a firework display or an exhibition of conjuring. His attitude seemed to irritate her. She recovered suddenly and launched into another tirade.

"Here I come," she said, "as paying guest to be nursed back to health and strength from a state of neurasthenic prostration, and find myself left to the mercies of a common house-boy, a nasty, common, low, little rapscallion like you – find myself literally *murdered* by neglect, but I'll sue you for damages, the whole *lot* of you – the doctor and the housemaid and the cook and you – you nasty little – *monkey* . . . and I'll have you all hung for murder."

She burst into tears again and William continued to watch her, not at all stung by her reflections on his personal appearance and social standing. He was hoping that the sobbing would lead to another fit of hysterics. It didn't, however. She dried her tears suddenly and sat up.

"It's more than an hour and a half," she said pathetically, "since I had any nourishment at all. The effect on my nervous system will be serious. My nerves are in such a condition that I must have nourishment every hour, every hour at least. Go and get me a glass of milk at once, boy."

William obligingly went downstairs and looked for some milk. He couldn't find any. At last he came upon a bowl of some milky-looking liquid. Much relieved he filled a glass with it and took it upstairs to the golden-haired lady. She received it with a suffering expression and, closing her eyes, took a dainty sip. Then her suffering expression changed to one of fury and she flung the glass of liquid at William's head. It missed William's head and emptied itself over a Venus de Milo by the door, the glass, miraculously unbroken, encaging the beauty's

117

head and shoulders. William watched this phenomenon with delight.

"You little fiend!" screamed the lady, "it's *starch!*"

"Starch," said William. "Fancy! An' it looked jus' like milk. But I say, it's funny about that glass stayin' on the stachoo like that. I bet you couldn't have done that if you'd tried!"

The lady had returned to her expression of patient suffering. She spoke with closed eyes and in a voice so faint that William could hardly hear it.

"I must have some nourishment at once. I've had nothing – *nothing* – since my breakfast at nine and now it's nearly eleven. And for my breakfast I only had a few eggs. Go and make me some cocoa at once . . . at once."

William went downstairs again and looked for some cocoa. He found a cupboard with various tins and in one tin he found a brown powder which might quite well be cocoa, though there was no label on it. Ever hopeful, he mixed some with water in a cup and took it up to the lady. Again she assumed her suffering expression, closed her eyes, and sipped it daintily. Again her suffering expression changed to one of fury, again she flung the cup at William and again she missed him. This time the cup hit a bust of William Shakespeare. Though the impact broke the cup the bottom of it rested hat-wise at a rakish angle upon the immortal bard's head, giving him a rather debauched appearance while the dark liquid streamed down his smug countenance.

"It's knife powder," screamed the lady hysterically. "Oh, you murderous little *brute*. It's knife powder! This will be the death of me. I'll never get over this as long as I live – never, *never,* NEVER!"

William stood expectant, awaiting the incvitable attack of hysterics. But it did not come. The lady's eyes had wandered to the window and there they stayed, growing wider and wider and rounder and rounder and wider, while her mouth slowly opened to its fullest extent. She pointed with a trembling hand.

"Look!" she said. "The river's flooding."

William looked. The part of the garden which could be seen from the window was completely under water. Then – and not till then – did William remember the hose pipe which he had left playing at full force in the back yard. He gazed in silent horror.

"I always *said* so," panted the lady hysterically, "I *said* so. I said so to Dr Morlan. I said, 'I couldn't live in a house in a valley. There'd be floods and my nerves couldn't stand them,' and he said that the river couldn't possibly flood this house and it can and I might have known he was lying and oh my poor nerves, what shall I do, what *shall* I do?"

William gazed around the room as if in search of inspiration. He met the gaze of Venus de Milo soaked in milk and leering through her enclosing glass; he met the gaze of William Shakespeare soaked in water and knife powder and wearing his broken cup jauntily. Neither afforded him inspiration.

"It rises as I watch it – inch by inch," shrilled the lady, "*inch* by *inch!* It's terrible . . . we're marooned . . . Oh, it's horrible. There isn't even a life belt in the house."

William was conscious of a great relief at her explanation of the spreading sheet of water. It would for the present at any rate divert guilt from him.

"Yes," he agreed looking out with her upon the water-covered garden. "That's what I bet it is – it's the river rising."

"Why didn't you *tell* me?" she screamed, "you must have known. Why, now I come to think of it, you were dripping wet when you first came into the room."

"Well," said William with a burst of inspiration, "I din' want to give you a sudden shock – what I thought it might give you tellin' you you was macarooned—"

"Oh, don't *talk*," she said. "Go down at once and see if you can find any hope of rescue."

William went downstairs again. He waded out to the hose pipe and wrestled again with the tap beneath the gushing water. In vain. He waded into a neighbouring shed and found three or four panic-stricken hens. He captured two and took them up to the lady's room, flinging them in carelessly.

"Rescued 'em," he said with quiet pride, and then went down for the others. The mingled sounds of the squeaking and terrified flight of hens and the lady's screams pursued him down the stairs. He caught the other two hens and brought them up, too, carelessly flinging them in to join the chaos. Then he went down for further investigations. In another shed he found a puppy who had climbed into a box to escape the water and there was engaged in trying to catch a spider on the wall. William rescued the puppy, and took it upstairs to join the lady's menagerie.

"Rescued this, too," he said as he deposited it inside.

It promptly began to chase the hens. There ensued a scene of wild confusion as the hens, with piercing squawks, flew over chairs and tables, pursued by the puppy.

Even the lady seemed to feel that hysterics would have no chance of competing with this uproar, so she began to chase the puppy. William returned to the deluge in which he was beginning to find an irresistible fascination. He had read a story not long ago in which a flood figured largely and in which the hero had rescued children and animals from the passing torrent and had taken them to a place of safety at the top of the house. In William's mind the law of association was a strong one. As he gazed upon the surging stream he became the rescuer hero of the story and began to look round for something else to rescue. There appeared to be no more livestock to be rescued from the sheds. He waded down to the road, which also was now partially under water, and looked up and down. A small pig had wandered out of a neighbouring farm and was standing contemplating the flooded road with interest and surprise. The hero rescuer of William's story had rescued a pig. Without a moment's hesitation William waded up to the pig, seized it firmly round the middle before it could escape, and staggered through the deluge with it and into the house. Though small, it showed more resistance than William had expected. It wriggled and squeaked and kicked in all directions. Panting, William staggered upstairs with it. He flung open the door and deposited the pig on the threshold.

"Here's somethin' else I've rescued," he said proudly.

The lady was showing unexpected capabilities in dealing with the situation. She had taken the china out of the china cabinet and had put the hens into it.

They were staring through the glass doors in stupid amazement and one of them had just complicated matters by laying an egg.

The lady was just disputing the possession of a table runner with the spirited puppy, who thought she was having a game with it. The puppy had already completely dismembered a hassock, a mat and two cushions. Traces of them lay about the room. Venus and Shakespeare, still wearing their rakish head adornments, were gazing at the scene through runnels of starch and liquid knife powder. Miss Polliter received the new refugee in a business-like fashion. She had evidently finally decided that this was no occasion for the display of nervous systems.

She seemed, in fact, exhilarated and stimulated.

"Put him down here," she said. "That's quite right, my boy. Go and rescue anything else you can. This is a noble work, indeed."

The puppy charged the pig and the pig charged the china cabinet. There came the sound of the breaking of glass. The egg rolled out and the puppy fell upon it with wild delight. The hens began to fly about the room in panic again.

William hastily shut the door and went downstairs to continue his work of rescuing. He had by this time almost persuaded himself that the flood was of natural origin and that he was performing heroic deeds of valour in rescuing its victims. Again he looked up and down the road. He felt that he had done his duty by the animal creation and he would have welcomed a rescuable human being.

Suddenly he saw two infants from the Infants School coming hand in hand down the road. They stared in amazement at the flood that barred their progress. Then with a touching faith in their power over the forces of nature and an innate love of paddling, they walked serenely into the midst of the stream. When they reached the middle, however, panic overcame them. The smaller one sat down and roared and the larger one stood on tip-toe and screamed. William at once plunged into the stream

124

and "rescued" them. They were stalwart infants but he managed to get one tucked under each arm and carried them roaring lustily and dripping copiously up to Miss Polliter's room. Again Miss Polliter had restored as if by magic a certain amount of order. She had cooped up the hens by an ingenious arrangement of the fireguard and she had put the pig in the coal scuttle, leaving him an air-hole through which he was determinedly squeezing the rest of him. The puppy had dealt thoroughly with the table runner while Miss Polliter was engaged on the hens and the pig, and was now seeing whether he could pull down window curtains or not.

William deposited his dripping, roaring infants.

"Some more I've rescued," he said succinctly.

Miss Polliter turned to him a face which was bright with interest and enterprise.

"Splendid, dear boy," she said happily, "splendid . . . I'll soon have them warmed and dried – or wait – is the flood rising?"

William said it was.

"Well, then, the best thing would be to go to the very top of the house where we shall be safer than here!"

Determinedly she picked up the infants, went out on to the landing and mounted the attic stairs. William followed, holding the puppy who managed during the journey to tear off and (presumably – as they were never seen again) swallow his pocket flap and three buttons from his coat. Then Miss Polliter returned for the pig and William followed with a hen. The pig was very recalcitrant and Miss Polliter said "Naughty," to him quite sternly once or twice. Then they returned for the other hens. One hen escaped and in the intoxication of sudden liberty flew squawking loudly out of a skylight.

In the attic bedroom where Miss Polliter now assembled her little company of refugees she lit the gas fire and started her great task of organization.

"I'll dry these dear children first," she said. "Now go down, dear boy, and see if there is anyone else in need of your aid."

William went downstairs slowly. Something of his rapture and excitement was leaving him. Cold reality was placing its icy grip upon his heart. He began to wonder what would happen to him when they discovered the nature and cause of his "flood", and whether the state to which the refugees were reducing the house would also be laid to his charge. He waded out to the hose pipe and had another fruitless struggle with the tap. Then he looked despondently up and down the road. The "flood" was spreading visibly, but there was no one in sight. He returned slowly and thoughtfully to Miss Polliter.

Miss Polliter looked brisk and happy. She had apparently forgotten both her nervous system and its need of perpetual nourishment. She was having a game with the infants who were now partially dried and crowing with delight. She had managed to drive the hens into a corner of the room and had secured them there by a chest of drawers. She had tied the pig by a piece of string to the wash-hand-stand and it was now lying down quite placidly, engaged in eating the carpet. One hen had escaped from its "coop" and was running round a table pursued by or pursuing (it was impossible to say which) the puppy. Miss Polliter was playing pat-a-cake with the drying infants and seemed to be enjoying it as much as the infants. She greeted William gaily.

"Don't look so sad, dear boy," she said. "I think that even though the river continues to rise all night we shall be safe here – quite safe here – and I daresay you can find something for these dear children to eat when they get hungry. I don't need anything. I'm quite all right. I can easily go without anything till morning. Now do one more thing for me, dear boy. Go down to my room on the lower floor and see the time. Dr Morlan said that he would be home by six."

Still more slowly, still more thoughtfully, William descended to her room on the lower floor and saw the time. It was five minutes to six. Dr Morlan might arrive then at any minute. William considered the situation from every angle. To depart now as unostentatiously as possible seemed to him a far, far better thing than to wait and face Dr Morlan's wrath. The hose pipe was damaged, the garden was flooded. Miss Polliter's room was like a battlefield after a battle, strange infants and a pig were disporting themselves about the house, a destructive puppy had wreaked its will upon every cushion and curtain and chair within reach (it had found that it could pull down window curtains).

William very quietly slipped out of the front door and crept down the drive. The flood seemed to be concentrating itself upon the back of the house. The front was still more or less dry. William crept across the field to the stile that led to the main road. Here his progress was barred by a group of three who stood talking by the stile. There was a tall pompous-looking man with a beard, a small woman and an elderly man.

"Oh, yes, we've quite settled in now," the tall, pompous-looking man was saying. "We've got a resident patient with us – a Miss Polliter who is a chronic nervous case. We are rather uneasy at having to leave her all today with only the cook and house-boy. Unfortunately our housemaid left us suddenly yesterday but we trust that things will have gone all right. An aunt of mine was reported to be seriously ill and we had to hurry to her to be in time but unfortunately – ahem – I mean fortunately – we found that she had taken a turn for the better so we returned as soon as we could."

"Of course," said the woman, "we'd have been back *ever* so much earlier if it hadn't been for that affair at the cave."

"Oh, yes," said the doctor, "very tragic affair, very tragic indeed. Some poor boy . . . there were a lot of people there trying to recover the body and they wanted to have a doctor in the unlikely case of the boy being still alive when they got him out. I assured them that it was very unlikely that he would be alive and that I had to get back to my own patient . . . and it would only be a matter of a few minutes to send for me . . . The poor mother was distraught."

"What had happened?" said the other man.

"Some rash child had crawled into an opening in the rock and had not come out. He must have been suffocated. His friends waited for over an hour before they notified the parents and I am afraid that it is too late now. They have repeatedly called to him but there is no response. As I told them, there are frequently poisonous gases in the fissures of the rock and the poor child must have succumbed to them. So far all attempts to recover the body have been unsuccessful. They have just sent for men with pickaxes."

William's heart was sinking lower and lower. Crumbs! He'd quite forgotten the cave part of it. Crumbs! He'd quite forgotten that he'd left the Outlaws in the cave waiting for him. The house-boy and the cook and the silver cleaning and the hose pipe and the flood and Miss Polliter and the hens and the pig and the puppy and the infants had completely driven the cave and the Outlaws out of his head. Crumbs, wouldn't everybody be mad!

For William had learnt by experience that with a strange perversity parents who had mourned their children as lost or dead are generally for some reason best known to themselves intensely irritated to find that they have been alive and well and near them all the time. William had little hopes of being received by his parents with the joy and affection that should be given to one miraculously restored to them from the fissures of the rock. And just as he stood pondering his next step the doctor turned and saw him. He stared at him for a few minutes, then said, "Do you want me, my boy? Anything wrong? You're the new house-boy, aren't you?"

William realized that he was still wearing the overalls which the house-boy had given him. He gaped at the doctor and blinked nervously, wondering whether it wouldn't be wiser to be the new house-boy as the doctor evidently thought he was. The doctor turned to his wife.

"Er – it *is* the new house-boy, dear, isn't it?" he said.

"I *think* so," said his wife doubtfully. "He only came this morning, you know, and Cook engaged him, and I hardly had time to look at him, but I think he is . . . Yes, he's wearing our overalls. What's your name, boy?"

William was on the point of saying "William Brown", then stopped himself. He mustn't be William Brown. William Brown was presumably lost in the bowels of the earth. And he didn't know the house-boy's name. So he gaped again and said:

"I don't know."

There came a gleam into the doctor's eye.

"What do you mean, my boy," he said. "Do you mean that you've lost your memory?"

"Yes," said William, relieved at the simplicity of the explanation, and the fact that it relieved him of all further responsibility. "Yes, I've lost my memory."

"Do you mean you don't remember anything?" said the doctor sharply.

"Yes," said William happily, "I don' remember anythin'."

"Not where you live or anything?"

"No," said William very firmly, "not where I live nor anything."

The other man, feeling evidently that he could contribute little illumination to the problem, moved on, leaving the doctor and his wife staring at William. They held a whispered consultation. Then the doctor turned to William and said suddenly:

"Frank Simpkins . . . does that suggest anything to you?"

"No," said William with perfect truth.

"Doesn't know his own name," whispered the doctor, then again sharply:

"Acacia Cottage . . . does that convey anything to you?"

"No," said William again with perfect truth.

The doctor turned to his wife.

"No memory of his name or home," he commented. "I've always wanted to study a case of this sort at close quarters. Now, my good boy, come back home with me."

But William didn't want to go back home with him. He didn't want to return to the house which still bore traces of his recent habitation and where his "flood" presumably still raged. He was just contemplating precipitate flight when a woman came hurrying along the road. The doctor's wife seemed to recognize her. She whispered to the doctor. The doctor turned to William.

"You know this woman, my boy, don't you?"

"No," said William, "I've never seen her before."

The doctor looked pleased. "Doesn't remember his own mother," he said to his wife, "quite an interesting case."

The woman approached them aggressively. The doctor stepped in front of William.

"Come after my boy," she said. "Sayin' 'is hours ended at five an' then keepin' 'im till now! I'll 'ave the lor on you, I will. Where is 'e?"

"Prepare yourself, my good woman," said the doctor, "for a slight shock. Your son has temporarily – only temporarily, we trust – lost his memory."

She screamed.

"What've you bin doin' of to 'im?" she said indignantly, "'e 'adn't lorst it when 'e left 'ome this mornin'. Where is 'e, anyway?"

Silently the doctor stepped on to one side, revealing William.

"Here he is," he said pompously.

"'Im?" she shrilled. "Never seen 'im before."

They stared at each other for some seconds in silence. Then William saw the real house-boy coming along the road and spoke with the hopelessness of one who surrenders himself to Fate to do its worst with.

"Here he is."

The real original house-boy was stepping blithely down the road, an extemporized rod over his shoulder, swinging precariously a jar full of minnows. He was evidently ignorant of the flight of time. He saw William first and called out cheerfully:

"I say, I've not been long, have I? Is it all right?"

Then he saw the others and the smile dropped from his face. His mother darted to him protectively.

"Oh, my pore, blessed child," she said, "what have they bin a-doin' to you – keepin' you hours an' hours after your time an' losin' your pore memory an' you your pore widowed mother's only child . . . Come home with your mother, then, an' she'll take care of you and we'll have the lor on them, we will."

The boy looked from one to another bewildered, then realizing from his mother's tones that he had been badly treated he burst into tears and was led away by his consoling parent.

The doctor and his wife turned to William for an explanation. Their expressions showed considerably less friendliness than they had shown before. William looked about him desperately. Even escape seemed impossible. He felt that he would have welcomed any interruption. When, however, he saw Miss Polliter running towards them down the field he felt that he would have chosen some other interruption than that.

"Oh, there you are!" panted Miss Polliter. "Such *dreadful* things have happened. Oh, there's the dear boy. I don't know what we should have done without him . . . rescuing children and animals at the risk, I'm sure, of his own dear life. I must give you just a little present." She handed him a half-crown which William pocketed gratefully.

"But, my dear Miss Polliter," said the doctor, deeply concerned, "you should be resting in your room. You should never run like that in your state of nervous exhaustion . . . never."

"Oh, I'm quite well now," said Miss Polliter.

"Well?" said the doctor amazed and horrified at the idea.

"Oh, yes," said Miss Polliter, "I feel ever so well. The flood's cured me."

"The flood?" said the doctor still more amazed and still more horrified.

"Oh yes. The river's risen and the whole place is flooded out," said Miss Polliter excitedly. "It's a most stimulating experience altogether. We've saved a lot of animals and two children."

The doctor was holding his head.

"Good Heavens!" he said. "Good Heavens! Good Heavens!"

At that moment two more women descended upon

the group. They were the mothers of the infants. They had searched through the village for their missing offspring and at last an eye-witness had described their deliberate kidnapping and imprisonment in the doctor's house. They were demanding the return of their children. They were threatening legal proceedings. They were calling the doctor a murderer and a kidnapper, a vivisectioner, a Hun and a Bolshevist.

The doctor and the doctor's wife and Miss Polliter and the two mothers all began to talk at once. William, seizing his opportunity, crept away. He crept down towards the cave.

At the bend in the road he turned. The doctor and the doctor's wife and the two mothers and Miss Polliter, still all talking excitedly at the same time, began to make their way slowly up the hill to the doctor's house.

He looked in the other direction. There was a large crowd surrounding the cave; men were just coming along the road from the other direction with pickaxes to dig his dead body from the rock.

He went forward very reluctantly and slowly.

He went forward because he had a horrible suspicion that the doctor would soon have discovered the extent and the cause of the "flood" and would soon be pursuing him lusting for vengeance.

He went forward reluctantly and slowly because he did not foresee an enthusiastic welcome from his bereaved parents.

Ginger saw him first. Ginger gave a piercing yell and pointed down the road towards William's reluctant form.

"There – he *is!*" he shouted. "He's not dead."

They all turned and gaped at him open-mouthed.

William presented a strange figure. He seemed at first sight chiefly compounded of the two elements, earth and water.

He turned as if to flee but the figure of the doctor could be seen running down the road from his house after him; following the doctor were the doctor's wife, the infants' mothers with the infants and Miss Polliter. Even at that distance he could see that the doctor's face was purple with fury. Miss Polliter still looked bright and stimulated.

So William advanced slowly towards his gaping rescuers. "Here I am," he said. "I – I've got out all right."

He fingered the half-crown in his pocket as if it were an amulet against disaster.

He felt that he would soon need an amulet against disaster.

"Oh, where have you been?" sobbed his mother, "where *have* you been?"

"I got in a flood," said William, "an' then I lost my memory." He looked round at the doctor who was running towards them and added with a mixture of fatalistic resignation and bitterness, "Oh, well, he'll tell you about it. I bet you'll b'lieve him sooner than me an' I bet he'll make a different tale of it to what I would."

And he did.

But Miss Polliter (who left the doctor's charge, cured, to his great disgust, the next day) persisted to her dying day that the river had flooded and that the hose pipe had nothing to do with it.

And she sent William a pound note the next week in an envelope marked "For a brave boy".

And, as William remarked bitterly, he jolly well deserved it . . .

Sniff Finds a Seagull

Ian Whybrow

I was wondering how you say in French, "The dog in our kitchen has got hazelnut spread and feathers on." I could do the first bit all right and I was just thinking to myself that there probably wasn't any French for the rest of it, when I heard Tom's mum scream. This was partly because there *was* a dog in the kitchen with hazelnut spread and feathers on. I was watching him through my periscope, so I should know.

It was a good periscope . . . worked really well. I could see brilliantly into the kitchen from outside on the patio. OK, I could have just looked without using the periscope, but then I could have been seen from indoors. The whole point of a periscope is to look round corners or over things without being seen, so, as I say, this one was dead good. I'd been watching for about five minutes actually. I'd told Mum that I'd keep an eye on my little sister Sal and her friend Tom while she and Tom's mum, Bunty, were upstairs looking at this wardrobe Mum had just bought at an auction. They were trying to decide whether to strip it or stencil it. I would have chucked it out, but there you are. So I sat at the garden table on the patio and got on with finishing my periscope while Sal and Tom mucked about with a couple of Transformer toys that Tom had brought with him. Sniff had disappeared somewhere.

Sal and Tom enjoyed themselves in their little kiddie way for a bit. They bent the Transformers about and didn't seem to mind if they didn't quite turn into guns or robots. Then they ran up and down on the patio going, "Do diss!" and "Look at me!" and then Sal chucked her Transformer at Tom and said, "I can frow diss!" Tom thought that was a good idea and threw his Transformer as far as he could off the patio on to the lawn. Sal picked hers up and did the same thing. Then they jumped down off the patio and picked up the Transformers and ran back up the two steps and chucked them off again.

The great thing was that while they were whizzing about, they didn't keep coming over to see what I was doing, so I could get on with making the periscope. I'd seen them making one on telly but I reckoned I could improve on it by using masking tape instead of Sellotape and by fitting a little mechanism for altering the angles of the mirrors. I'd had a bit of trouble and several goes at getting the case just right but I cracked the problem just when I thought I was running out of breakfast cereal packets.

I'd just about got it finished when Sal and Tom got fed up with the garden and headed for the kitchen. Handy, because now I could test whether it really worked.

I knelt on the patio, under the window. I could hear cupboard doors being opened and closed. I guessed what was going on and I brought the periscope up to my eye to check my theory. Brilliant! I could see everything . . . and there was little Sal dragging a chair up under the cupboard where the jam's kept. She was after the hazelnut spread. The conversation went something like this:

Sal: "I like some haysnut sped. You like some haysnut sped, Tom?"
Tom: "Nahh."
Sal: "It in nat cupboard." (Climbs on chair.) "I get some for you."
Tom: "Dome wannenny."
Sal: "Here it is. In nis cupboard. Want some? Snice."
Tom: "Nahh."
Sal: (Climbing down with large tub.) "Can you take da lid off, Tom? I can. Look. Dass easy."

Tom: "Wass dat?"

Sal: "Dass haysnut sped. Dass nice. Here, open you mowff. Nice?"

Tom: "*Ppppppththppp.*"

Sal: "Don't you like it? Snice."

At that point, Sal dipped her fingers into the tub, put a handful of the gooey stuff into her own mouth and went *Ppppppththppp* because that's what Tom had done. Hazelnut spread spattered over the nearby cupboard doors and on to the floor. Then Tom dipped his fingers into the tub, scooped out some gunge and let Sal have another go. Sal took her turn to scoop some into Tom's mouth. This went on for a bit and then Sniff brought in the dead seagull.

He quite often brings in things if he finds them lying around . . . bones, shoes, sticks, old tennis balls, that sort of thing. He brought in a dried cowpat once. He likes smelly things. I think that's why he brought in the seagull. Anyway, as soon as he saw the hazelnut spread, he lost interest in the seagull and dropped it on the kitchen floor. And as soon as Sal and Tom saw the seagull, they lost interest in the hazelnut spread. They changed places and started exploring.

Sniff didn't usually get a proper go at the hazelnut spread and normally had to rely on licking Sal after

she'd had some. So he was obviously very interested in the tub and got his head in as far as he could. Likewise, being too noisy and scary to get very close to a real live seagull, Sal and Tom must have thought that *they* were dead lucky to have a chance with this one that Sniff had found, especially as it didn't mind them having a close look at its feathers.

That was how there came to be such a lot of feathers and hazelnut spread on the floor and the cupboard doors and the dog and on Sal and Tom. And it wasn't long after that that Bunty came in and let out a scream that was surprising for a grown-up woman.

"Tommy! Sally! What on earth is going on?" she

wailed. "And oh, good grief! What is THAT?"

"It looks like a seagull," said Mum. "And . . . err!" she clamped her hanky to her nose. "It smells as if it's been dead for a week."

Sniff thought he was being congratulated for bringing in something really ace. Wagging the old tail into a fan that wafted a feathery cloud into the air, he darted forward and grabbed the seagull, growling playfully. He jumped up at Mum, planting his sticky great paws on her skirt and his sticky great face in her chest and offering her his prize.

"Get down, Sniff! Sniff, down! No, I don't want that. No!"

"Me have it," said Sal, stepping forward.

Bunty grabbed her and hauled her up into the air as if she was snatching her from a minefield. Naturally, quite a bit of what had been sticking to Sal transferred to Tom's mum.

Meanwhile, my mum had got the back door open and was pointing outwards towards the distant horizon, calling "Out! Out!" When that didn't work she got the mop out and half-scooped, half-pushed Sniff into the garden and slammed the door after him.

Sal and Tom squealed furiously. I don't think they were shocked at the treatment Sniff had received from Mum. Actually, they were cheesed off that he'd pinched the seagull they'd been stopped from playing with. Now he was galloping off, down to the field to bury it somewhere near where he'd found it. As I watched him pounding off through the hole in the fence at the bottom of the garden, leaving a few white feathers stuck to the fencing boards on either side of the gap, I wondered what a stranger might think as they saw him galumphing along, fur and feathers waving together in the breeze. Headline: BIRDBEAST CAUSES RIOT ON RECREATION FIELD — TOWNSFOLK FLEE.

"Where's Ben?" said Mum in a voice that got Sal's attention and mine, even though I was outside.

"In da garding."

"Stupid boy! What's he doing out there? He is supposed to be keeping an eye on you two little terrors! Now look at you. And this place. And me!"

"And me!" added Bunty. "I am covered in gunk! What *is* this stuff?"

"Haysnut sped," said Tom, who now knew. "Snice."

"And fevvers," added Sal.

"I don't know about hazelnut – but it certainly does spread," said Bunty. (Dead witty.) "It's spread all over this kitchen. How could two little kids make a mess like this in five minutes?"

"Not me and Tom," said Sal, shaking her head seriously. "Niff done dat."

"Nahh," agreed Tom, who meant "yeah" but didn't like saying it.

"And I know just the person to clean it all up," said Mum. "Ben!"

It was no good me explaining that I *was* keeping my eye on them. Never mind that I didn't take my eye off them. That didn't seem to count. No. I am irresponsible. I am a pain. I have no consideration for others. And I can blinking well clear up the whole sticky, revolting mess. And if I think I'm going out enjoying myself that afternoon, I've got another think coming. All that.

Took me ages to get that place cleaned up. *And* I had to wipe up stuff that wasn't even feathers or hazelnut spread.

It wasn't until Dad came in hours later that anyone showed the least bit of interest in my periscope, either. He thought it was great – and might come in handy for finding things that had rolled under washing machines and sideboards and stuff like that. I think what really finished Mum off was that I'd cut up all the cereal boxes to make the case, so that the raisin bran and the muesli and the Shreddies and the Wheetos all got mixed up together in the cake tin I tipped them in. That's the trouble with this country, not enough people appreciate the scientific spirit. It could be a genius staring them in the face – and all they can see are a few seagull feathers, a mucked-about muesli and a splash or two of hazelnut spread.

Still, I must say we all had a laugh later on when Sniff came creeping back for his supper and we pounced on him and gave him a bath. But that's another story.

A Work of Art

Margaret Mahy

Mrs Baskin's big son, Brian, was working in another city, but he was coming home for his birthday, so she decided to make him a rich fruitcake and to ice it herself. She had been taking cake-icing lessons at the Polytech for nearly a year and by now she felt she was rather good at it, better indeed than her instructor, who liked brightly coloured, frilly sort of icing. Mrs Baskin preferred something plainer and cooler. As she got out the cake mixing bowl, wooden spoon, a big plastic bowl for the dried fruit, the sifter for sifting the dry ingredients, as well as the big, hinged cake-tin, a picture came into her mind of how the cake might look: pure, almost – but not quite – unearthly, a cake that had been iced by moonlight on midsummer night. She looked at her calendar and saw with pleasure that it would be full moon that night.

Mrs Baskin set about things in a very orderly

fashion. First she greased one side of the greaseproof paper with a knob of butter, and then she fitted it, butterside up, in the big, hinged cake-tin. She turned on the oven so that it would be heating while she worked. Then she put the dried fruit into the plastic bowl – currants, candied peel, sultanas, seedless raisins, a little bit of chopped ginger and almonds, as well as glacé cherries and crystallized angelica to give a bit of colour to the cake when it was sliced. Once she'd mixed the dried fruit, she floured it a little so the fruit wouldn't stick to itself. Then she sifted half a pound of plain flour and half a teaspoon of baking powder into yet another bowl, an old pottery one that had belonged to her mother.

Her three youngest children, Hamlet, Serena and Toby, watched her, for they were as interested in Brian's cake as if it were theirs too. They were certain Brian would let them have some of it. Even Wellington, the dog, watched, wagging his tail whenever anyone spoke to him. Hubert, the cat, pretended to be asleep, but if you looked closely you could see two thin, green slits in his black face. He liked to know just what was going on in his house.

Mrs Baskin creamed butter and brown sugar until the mixture was light and fluffy, and then beat in four eggs, one at a time. She slowly added the flour, stirring as she went, and finally the fruit mixture.

Her arm grew rather tired. Hamlet had a go, but he could scarcely move the spoon. Serena had a go, but she couldn't move it at all. Toby was too little even to try. He could barely stand, let alone stir a birthday cake. Not only that, he was teething and Mrs Baskin thought he might dribble into the mixture. Of course, Wellington and Hubert were no use at all.

Just then, the big girls, Audrey and Vanilla, came in from school, arguing and hitting each other with their school bags. But they stopped fighting when they saw that their mother was making a birthday cake. They quickly realized that there would be delicious cake mixture left on the inside of the mixing bowl.

"Mum, Mum, can I lick the bowl?" they cried together.

There was an immediate rush for the spoon drawer. Everyone but Toby grabbed a spoon. Mrs Baskin carefully scraped most of the mixture into her hinged cake-tin and put it in the oven.

At that moment one of the middle boys, Leonard, came in from cricket practice. Mrs Baskin gave him the mixing spoon to lick. Audrey said it wasn't fair. Vanilla said Serena was letting her hair drag in the bowl. Serena hit Hamlet with her spoon for taking too much. Hamlet pretended he was badly hurt, fell over backwards and knocked Toby over.

Immediately, Wellington stood on everyone and began licking the bowl before anyone else.

After she had baked the cake for an hour and a half, Mrs Baskin lowered the oven temperature and baked it for a further two and a quarter hours. By the time it was ready to come out of the tin the other middle boy, Greville, came in. The bowl and the mixing spoon were washed and put away by then, but Greville didn't care. He had had a secret meal of fish and chips with his friend Simon, under Simon's bed. He liked the look of the cake though, and said he couldn't wait for Brian to get home.

When the cake was properly cool, Mrs Baskin brushed it with apricot glaze before covering it in almond paste. Then she drove Greville away from the television (the six youngest children were already in bed), made herself a cup of tea, turned the television off, and sat in the moony dark for a little while, getting herself into a magic, cake-icing mood. She had a short, refreshing sleep, then got up, washed her face and put on some make-up (so as to get in a birthday party mood). She thought about Brian who had been her first baby. She thought about him growing year by year, losing teeth, scraping his knees, learning how to ride a bike, going to college, and so on. The cake needed to be iced in such a way that anyone who saw it would somehow be aware of these things. She would not write *Happy Birthday* on it but she would ice it so that anyone who saw it would *feel* Happy Birthday-ish.

While she iced, the moon peered in at the window, looking rather like an iced cake itself. Mrs Baskin smiled and waved to it. She thought it looked surprised but pleased. When she had finished icing the cake she put it on a silver stand and then, because it seemed a pity to shut it away in a cake-tin, she covered it with a glass dome which had once belonged to her grandmother, and stood it on top of the piano. The moon looked in and touched it gently. The cake seemed to glow with a moony light of its own.

When the children saw the cake next morning they all stood and stared at it, astonished.

"Gee, Mum, it's too good to eat," said Greville, though he didn't really mean it.

The children who were old enough to go to school went to school; the little children played under the table. Mrs Baskin began to vacuum the house. The vacuum cleaner made a lot of noise and she did not hear the knock at the door, but Hamlet heard it. He opened the door and let two men in. One was dressed in a floppy, striped shirt and designer-jeans. The other wore an elegant suit.

"Excuse us," they said, "but we are the owners of the art gallery down the road. We just happened to

be passing and we saw that wonderful thing you have there on your piano. Is it yours?"

Mrs Baskin explained that it was hers in a way. She had made it. However, the real owner was her son, Brian, who would be coming home in a month's time.

"It's a very rich cake," she explained, "and it will improve over the next month. Cakes like these improve with keeping."

The gallery owners, who were both on permanent diets, did not know much about cakes. They were astonished to find the elegant sculpture they had admired through the window was actually an iced birthday cake.

"It has a certain look, a certain ambience . . . I don't know! What would you say, Wynstan?" asked the one in the striped, floppy shirt, whose own name was Zachary.

"Purity!" said Wynstan. "What do you say, Zack? Shall we make an offer?"

They offered Mrs Baskin fifty dollars for her cake. She was certainly tempted. But it would not be full moon again for a month, and she had iced that cake at that special time in that special way for Brian. If she sold it she knew she could not make another one quite as good until it was full moon again.

"I'll rent it to you for fifty dollars," she said at last. "But you must get it insured against anyone eating it and you mustn't take it from under the glass dome or it'll get dusty."

She didn't think they would take her up on her offer but, after a lot of frowning and arguing, they did. There was something about that cake – they couldn't quite say what it was – but they were determined to display it in their gallery. They came round with a van later in the day and carried it off.

When the little ones saw the cake being carried off, they all began to cry. Mrs Baskin told them that it would be coming back again but they did not believe her. They were sure the gallery owners would take the cake into their gallery and then eat it all themselves. Being so small they didn't understand that it was insured.

The next morning on the front page of the newspaper, there was a photograph of Mrs Baskin's cake. *Tour de force by Local Artist*, said a headline.

"It's not a *tour de force*," complained Audrey. "It's an iced cake."

"Gee, you're dumb," said Greville. "A *tour de force* means a – it means something terrific."

"You don't know what it means either!" said Vanilla, who always stuck up for Audrey when Audrey was arguing with Greville. Greville went into his room pretending he didn't care, and looked up *tour de force* in the dictionary.

155

"*Tour de force* means feat of strength or skill, you noddy!" he said when he came back.

"Mum, Greville's calling me a noddy!" complained Audrey.

"That means I've got two *tour de forces,*" said Leonard, dancing up and down. "Feet of skill and strength."

"Well, they smell pretty strong after you've been playing cricket," said Vanilla.

"That's enough of that," said Mrs Baskin. She had been trying to talk to someone on the phone. "Help me tidy the house! The television people are coming round."

The children were so impressed at the thought of being on television that they raced about helping their mother by turning cushions upside down so that the cat fur Hubert had left on them was underneath. But by half-past eight the cameras had still not arrived and the big children had to go to school.

Mrs Baskin wished she had had time to get her hair set, but it was too late. She tore into the bathroom and put on some lipstick and eyeliner to brighten herself up a bit. The television people came in, Wellington barked himself hoarse, while Hubert panicked and shot up the curtains to hide on top of the bookshelf.

"When did you get the idea of using cake as an art form?" asked the television interviewer. "Is it a feminist protest against being a slave in the kitchen?"

"No, it's a birthday cake," said Mrs Baskin. "My son, Brian, is coming home for his birthday next month and I made a cake for him."

Mrs Baskin was on television that night. Apart from her hair, she thought she did pretty well, but she wasn't the only person on the programme. There was a man from the local university talking about her cake.

"What we see here is a return to folk art . . . to the art of the *people*," he said. "It is functional art – this cake is meant to be *used*, and yet the artist shows instinctive awareness of texture and balance. She *interprets* the quality of *cakeness* and tests her creation against traditional concepts. Tradition is recognized, and yet I think we are witnessing the emergence of a new dynamic."

"Wow, Mum!" said Greville.

"Pretty cool!" said Vanilla. "But when are they going to bring that cake back?"

"Brian doesn't come home for a month," Mrs Baskin said. "That cake's probably safer there than it is here."

"You bet!" agreed Leonard, clashing his knife and

fork, which encouraged all the little ones to clash their knives and forks, too.

"Now then," said Mrs Baskin, "that's enough of that! You kids can do the dishes. I'm going out."

"Where are you going?" asked Audrey.

"Just down the road to the gallery," said Mrs Baskin. "Greville will babysit. You can put Toby to bed, Leonard! Read Hamlet a story, Vanilla!"

She put on her best dress and went down to the gallery. Her iced cake looked very beautiful, very mysterious, sitting in the window. It looked a little like a lot of different things, but most of all it looked like something simple which somehow nobody had ever noticed until now. It was the mixture of looking like a lot of other things and looking like something entirely new that made it so astonishing. As well as all that it was a cake. Everyone liked it.

When Mrs Baskin stepped into the gallery, Zack and Wynstan ran to meet her. Zack kissed her right hand and Wynstan kissed her left, and Wynstan's mother came to tell her how thrilling her cake was.

"When I saw it, I said, that's *art*! I said, that's what art's about. It's a cake – yes – but not *just* a cake. It's a statement in its own right. My dear, it's got such passionate equilibrium."

Mrs Baskin talked to a lot of interesting people in the gallery, drank some sherry and ate a slice of another, inferior cake. She enjoyed herself and was able to check that her cake was being well looked after. The gallery was dust free and had controlled humidity.

The next day she had her hair set, and it was just as well she did, for two reporters from art magazines came to talk to her, bringing photographers with them.

"I can't tell you how much I admire it," said one reporter. "The stand, the cake itself, and the dome, are all organized to make separate yet identical statements. You've somehow represented the finite universe, continuous in space, powerful in its defiance of causality, but threatened by entropy. And then there's the time dimension. Implicit in it are times we can define as *before cake* and *after cake*."

When they had gone, Mrs Baskin went down to the gallery again. She had to wait in a small queue that had formed in order to look at her cake. People stared through the glass longingly, and it took quite a while for the queue to move. At last it was Mrs Baskin's turn. As she filed past it she took a good, hard look at it. She saw that all the things the critics and reporters were saying could be quite true. She also saw that the cake was looking as fresh as ever and that there was no dust on it.

Over the next day or two Mrs Baskin received

phone calls from London and New York. Certain art galleries were anxious to display her cake. Others were flying art critics over to write about it.

Vanilla and Audrey quickly learned to talk like art critics.

"Audrey, what do you think of the sculptural projection of this sandwich?" Vanilla would ask.

"I think it's visually significant," Audrey would say. "But the tomato's sliding out of it!"

"I made it like that on purpose," Vanilla cried, catching the tomato. "To give it immediacy."

"Gee, what a pair of noddys!" exclaimed Leonard.

"Noddys!" repeated Hamlet, pleased to join in talking to the big ones.

"Mum, Leonard's teaching Hamlet to call us noddys," shouted Audrey and Vanilla together.

Three weeks later it was announced that Mrs Baskin had won a medal for a significant contribution to new art. The President of the Society of Arts presented the medal and shook her hand.

"What a cake!" he cried. "It has a certain Byzantine quality, no?"

"Maybe . . ." said Mrs Baskin. Once people had pointed out things about her cake to her she often saw them herself. Had they been there all the time? Or did people call them into being by naming them? And did it matter?

At the end of a fortnight there was a change of display at the gallery and her cake was sent home.

"But don't worry!" said Wynstan. "We have lots of openings for it. Let us be your agents: your cake has a brilliant career in front of it."

Never had his gallery been so full. Never had there been such queues or such enthusiasm. He and Zack were planning a great pikelet-and-jam exhibition. He could hear the critics now. "There is an effortless virtuosity about the way the jam is applied that takes the breath away," or, "The static alignment of the pikelet brings out the semi-fluid texture of the jam component."

He went home feeling very happy.

His mother had made him a pancake, not great art, but very tasty. Suddenly, the phone rang. Wynstan answered it. Within ten minutes he had leaped into his car and rushed around to get Zack. Within three minutes they were on their way to Mrs Baskin's.

They did not knock. They burst into her front room and found her among her children – Toby, Serena, Hamlet, Audrey, Vanilla, Leonard and Greville. But there was one other. A tall, young man sat there with Hubert on his knees and Wellington under his chair. Everyone had a very well-fed look.

Wynstan seized Mrs Baskin's hand.

"Wonderful news, dear!" he said. "I've just had a

Japanese firm on the phone and they want to buy your cake for ten thousand."

"Ten thousand what?" asked Mrs Baskin.

"Dollars, pounds, yen . . . who cares!" cried Zack. "We'll only take fifteen per cent commission and the rest of that lovely lolly will be yours. Where is the cake?"

Mrs Baskin pointed.

What was left of it was in the middle of the table. The cherries and the angelica glowed like rubies and emeralds among the dark, rich crumbs.

"You've eaten it!?" cried Wynstan. "You've eaten a work of art."

"We all did," said Brian (for the young man with Hubert on his knees was Brian). "It was my birthday cake!"

"But that wasn't just a cake. It was art!" cried Wynstan.

Mrs Baskin got up from the table.

"It was art," she agreed, "But it was also a cake – Brian's birthday cake. Some art is meant to last and some is meant to be eaten up. Not everything has to be a monument."

"It was terrific cake," said Brian. "Have some?"

Wynstan and Zack looked hungrily at the cake.

"Well, maybe just a crumb," said Zack, accepting a large slice. Later, both he and Wynstan had to admit it was the best-tasting art they had ever come across.

Mrs Baskin watched everyone enjoying the cake and thought of her big, hinged cake-tin, the plastic bowl, the pottery bowl, and the big mixing bowl waiting quietly in the dark cupboard, and a mysterious excitement stirred in her.

"I'll make another cake tomorrow . . . but not a birthday cake. You can't make the same cake twice," she thought to herself, and she glanced at the calendar. Four weeks had gone by surprisingly quickly. Tomorrow night the moon would be full again.

The Day I Died

Terry Tapp

It really was the most inconvenient time to die. Not that there is, I suppose, a truly convenient time for such things. But when I died, last Tuesday morning, I could have hoped for a sign, or some sort of warning. After all, I usually take my washing to the launderette on a Tuesday evening. But then, I would not be needing clean clothes, so perhaps it was better to save the money. (Although, having saved the money by *not* having to launder my clothes was frustrating too, for I never had the chance to spend the money I had just saved!)

Yes, dying can be a vexing affair, but I do realize that, for everyone, there is a time to live and a time to die. Given the choice (which I was not), I would have preferred to have finished my beef tea, and the fact that I had suddenly become unable to drink more than half a cupful of it was, to say the least of it, very disappointing.

One minute I was seated comfortably in my favourite chair in the staffroom; the next minute I was dead. I felt rather as one does when the film breaks at a cinema – sort of switched off and empty.

However, dying does have its good side, too. I was most fortunate in being spared the indignity of expiring whilst teaching Form 2C. It is not difficult to imagine the delight such a spectacular occasion would have caused the boys and girls of that class! Come to think of it, I had spent a considerable time during that last lesson bending over the aquarium, and it would have been a very messy business had I fallen head first into it! Young Andrew Smart would undoubtedly have come up with one of his usual witticisms. Come to that, had I been a few seconds later in completing my leave of this world, I am certain that the thick, ash cane which was gripped in the trembling hand of Mr Bassett would have fallen upon the posterior of young Mainwearing with devastating effect. So, I suppose, looking back on it, I rather timed everything quite well! But I digress, for I am describing my end before the story begins.

A few minutes before I died, I had been making my way along the corridor to the staffroom, ordering the children to "walk, not run" whilst inside the school building, as was my habit. Not that the running children ever took much notice of my orders, anyway, but they did at least slow down somewhat. Once inside the staffroom (a blessed oasis in the desert, away from noisy children!), I had seated myself in my favourite chair to wait for Mrs Simpkins (Domestic Science) to make my usual cup of hot beef tea. Mrs Simpkins makes an extraordinarily good cup of beef tea and I always looked forward to it enormously.

For a few minutes I enjoyed some friendly banter with my fellow teachers, and Mr Evans (History) asked me when I was thinking of retiring *again*. This caused much amusement, for, as they knew, I had already retired from teaching some five years ago, but each year I received a letter from our headmaster inviting me to apply for a position again. I must admit that having received a handsome clock and a cheque as a retiring present from the staff and pupils, I did feel rather fraudulent turning up for work each day! Mr Roper (Integrated Studies) was full of good humour that morning, and he suggested that I should retire every year and thus receive a clock and cheque each time.

As we chatted amiably, the door suddenly burst open and Mr Bassett, a red-faced young teacher with an unruly temper, came charging into the room, his fingers pinched, crablike, to the ear of young Mainwearing, whose face was contorted with pain.

"I'll teach you!" Bassett cried. "I'll teach you not to be rude to me in my classroom!" Bassett (Mathematics, by the way) dragged the child into the centre of the room and gave the ear an extra pinch for luck.

For myself, there is nothing I like better than a good book and a bag of clear mints at my side. Mr Evans plays golf, and Mr Roper is, I believe, a keen philatelist; Mrs Simpkins is, so I am told, an excellent knitter. Mr Bassett has no such outside interests and loves nothing better than to whisk his cane before the terrified eyes of an ashen-faced child before beating him thoroughly and without pity. A

strange fellow is Mr Bassett, and one whom I have not the slightest desire to befriend – not that I would now be capable of doing such a thing, anyway!

We must not, however, leave the poor child in suspense whilst I tell you about my likes and dislikes. The child, in this particular instance, was young Freddy Mainwearing, and I found it most surprising that this inoffensive little fellow should have fallen foul of Bassett, for the boy was usually well-mannered and, I would have thought, almost incapable of being rude. But then, when Mr Bassett was on the prowl, he was like a lion seeking for prey. And Mr Bassett usually managed to feed at least one child a day to the insatiable appetite of his brutal cane.

"Bend over that chair, you young hooligan!" Bassett roared. "I'm going to flog the living daylights out of you!" He selected his thickest cane from the staff cupboard and flexed it menacingly, bending it expertly until it was almost doubled over. (I had made a habit, in the past, of stealing a cane now and then from the cupboard, but Mr Bassett replenished his stock regularly.)

Freddy Mainwearing, having heard dreadful tales of the force with which Mr Bassett caned his victims, broke down at the sight of Bassett standing there. "I didn't mean to be rude, sir," he sobbed. "Honestly I didn't." He blinked his moist eyes owlishly behind his thick-lensed spectacles.

My heart went out to the lad, and had it been myself in charge of the matter I would have let him off with a severe caution. However, the matter was not in my hands, and Bassett took advantage of the situation to fuel his temper so that he could, when the cane fell, muster all the force in his body. "What?" he cried. "Are you being rude again? Who told you to speak, lad? Eh? Can't take your punishment like a man, eh? Is that it Main-Wearing?" He deliberately mispronounced the boy's name, spitting out the syllables with venom. "Well, we shall soon see what stuff you are made of. Bend over." Bassett removed his coat and checked that everyone in the staffroom was watching him. He loved nothing better than to make an exhibition of his brutality.

"Mannering," I said.

"Eh?" Bassett turned to face me. "What did you say?"

"The boy's name is pronounced 'Mannering', not 'Main-Wearing', Mr Bassett," I told him.

"That's what I was telling Mr Bassett, sir," said young Freddy tearfully. "I wasn't trying to be rude to him."

"Shut up!" Bassett yelled. "Heaven help us when you *are* trying to be rude, Main-Wearing! For a person who was *not* trying you have managed to be very rude indeed. I refuse to be corrected by a mere child!"

"Even when you are wrong, Mr Bassett?" I enquired mildly.

"What?" Bassett had lifted the cane above his head and stood there, poised, yet uncertain. "What are you talking about, Morgan?"

"If you have been guilty of making an error, and a child has pointed out that error to you, I do not think the child should be punished for doing so," I said. "Surely young Mainwearing is best qualified to know how to pronounce his own name?"

The cane wavered. Other masters were nodding their heads, and Mrs Simpkins, appalled by the sight of violence, had turned away, her hands over her eyes.

"He corrected me!" Bassett shouted. "Whether he is right or wrong is not the question. I will not be corrected in front of my class. It makes me look such a fool."

"And surely you would look even more foolish if you punished a child who was simply speaking the truth?" I asked. "May I ask you to postpone this boy's punishment whilst we discuss the matter over a cup of tea, in private?"

"Very sensible," said Mr Evans (History, if you

remember). "You need to cool down, Bassett, old chap."

"Wait outside," snarled Bassett. "When we have had our discussion I will be out there to beat the daylights out of you, Main-Wearing!"

Young Freddy left the room, an expression of terror and misery on his stricken face, and I was determined to intercede most strongly on his behalf. I was not, however, allowed the opportunity of doing so, for it was at that precise moment that I died.

It had been a peculiarity of my life that I am always the last person to know about important things which affect me. Why, only last week I was heartily congratulated on winning "The Neatest Garden in Brastonbury Award" at least two hours before I had been officially informed by the judges! Everyone had been aware of the award except me. The same situation existed when I died: I was the last one to learn of it.

Bassett had slammed the door hard behind young Mainwearing, then wheeled to face me, his expression menacing and hard. "I will not have you criticize my teaching methods before a child, Ernest Morgan!" he yelled. "What do you mean by interfering?"

"I mean to see that justice prevails," I told him quietly.

Evidently Bassett was not to be intimidated with such grand words. He stared at me, his mouth thin and cruel. "Well? Answer me, Morgan!"

"I have just this minute answered you," I replied. "But, if you wish me to particularize, then I am bound to say that I find you a brutal, uncaring fellow and—"

"Answer me!" Bassett screamed. "Don't just sit there like a statue." He bent over, staring intently into my eyes. "Have you suddenly gone deaf?"

"I can hear you perfectly," I replied, although I must admit that a strange feeling of warmth was now pervading my body. Bassett leaned closer, still staring, then was joined by Mr Evans and Mr Roper. They were all staring at me in a most peculiar manner.

"Is he deaf?" Bassett asked, his eyes still fixed upon my face.

"Of course I'm not!" I shouted.

Mr Evans shook his head. "No, he's not deaf. He's dead."

"Dead!" Bassett stepped smartly backwards.

"Deader than a door post," said Mr Evans.

"A door nail," I corrected. "The expression is 'dead as a door nail'."

They appeared not to be able to hear me, and Mr Roper, always a very practical man, lifted my wrist and felt for my pulse. It was an extremely unsettling experience to have one's wrist lifted, yet not feel anything.

"He's gone, all right," said Mr Roper, ignoring the fact that I was still there. He let my wrist drop into my lap, and I just sat there, watching it fall, unable to control it.

"Has he – passed over?" asked Mrs Simpkins tearfully.

"I am not an aeroplane," I interrupted, "and I certainly have not passed over."

"Yes," said Mr Roper. "Poor old Ernest is dead." And he made the statement with such authority that I was half inclined to believe him. Mr Roper has an authoritative way about him.

Mrs Simpkins stood before me, dewy-eyed, clutching an invisible bunch of flowers in her nervous, fluttering hands. A thin tearlet welled up into her left eye and she assisted its passage by squeezing it out on to her cheeks with a series of furious blinks.

It would, I think, have been regarded by her as a sin not to shed at least one tear on such an occasion, and she demonstrated her achievement noisily by searching in the sleeve of her voluminous cardigan and producing an immense paper tissue into which she trumpeted like an elephant. "A lovely man," she said, lapsing into her Welsh accent (a habit she was prone to when distressed). "An' him never finishing his tea, look you."

To confound their suspicions, I decided to demonstrate that I was alive, and well, by finishing off that delicious beef tea. Reaching out to take hold of the mug, I was amazed to see my hand pass straight through it! Come to that, my hand had a rather watery look about it – so watery in fact that I could see right through it! This phenomenon caused me so much surprise that I leaped from my chair with a cry. Yet no one appeared to be at all interested in my gymnastics, for they were still staring at the chair which I had just vacated. And no wonder – I had not vacated it! I was standing some four feet behind them, and they were staring at my lifeless body in awe. Now I know exactly what is meant by the expression "jumping out of one's skin", for that is precisely what I did!

My first thought was that I had no business leaving my body without permission and that I ought to jolly well thread myself back in again before I caught cold! But getting inside one's insides is rather more difficult than you can imagine. I sat on my own lap and pressed down as hard as I could, sinking through the still frame of my body, but it was not easy. Imagine trying to put on a stiff, one-piece suit of armour and you will have some idea of the problem.

As soon as I had comfortably threaded myself into my arms, my feet popped out through my knees, or my calves! Some moments of panic passed before I realized that I was exiled from my body and that I was, as everyone else had agreed, perfectly dead.

So what was I? Or, to be correct, what am I?

Mr Bassett soon accustomed himself to the situation and shrugged indifferently. He passed off my passing on and told everyone that he had better get back to his class.

Mrs Simpkins, afraid that she might be left alone in the staffroom with my lifeless body, made some excuse and rushed away. It was Mr Roper who decided that the undertaker should be telephoned and that I should be removed as quickly as possible so that the children would be unaware of what had happened until the headmaster could announce it in a dignified manner at the morning assembly. Gosh! It would be fun to turn up at the assembly and watch the expressions on their faces!

As they made arrangements for the discreet disposal of my remains, I came to terms with the fact that, apart from being unable to communicate with anyone, I was still the same Ernest Morgan. No – to tell the truth, I had become a new, improved Ernest

Morgan, for my aches and pains had entirely disappeared and I felt young and frisky as a lamb. When Mr Roper walked right through me, I was delighted with my new state. Invisible! Now I could see without being seen, and listen, too! Death is not at all the miserable experience it is presumed to be. On the contrary – I was enjoying it.

But I had not yet discovered the full extent of my powers. I started to hear voices, like whisperings in the mind (rather similar to tuning in a radio set). Soon I learned to tune into voices and could hear them quite clearly. The "voices" I heard were the innermost thoughts of people in the school buildings.

Travel presented no problems at all, for I merely had to think of a place, and I was there! For me, time, distance and all physical considerations had ceased to exist. For a while I remained with my body out of a sense of loyalty. Having lived within its narrow confines for so many years, I felt rather like a traitor deserting it now, although it was no use to me.

The undertakers came within minutes, sombre-faced, and set about their task, lifting my body into a polythene sack and placing it on a stretcher to take it out to the large, black car which had been parked discreetly by the door. Fortunately the children were not in the playground and no one, save the headmaster, witnessed my departure. I stood beside the headmaster as he waved a last farewell to the departing car. "Goodbye, Ernest, old fellow," he said under his breath. "We will all miss you most sadly."

I patted him on the shoulder, but my hand went through his clothes and his bones, and he did not hear me trying to comfort him. "Cheer up, Headmaster," I said. "Dying is rather fun, once you get used to the idea!"

Then I heard an insistent voice in my mind, loud and brutal. It was Bassett, shouting at his pupils. "You blithering idiots!" he was yelling. "I am going to drum this into your minds if it is the last thing I do."

Thinking of Bassett was enough to cause me to appear in his classroom instantly. He was standing by the blackboard, his face as red as an Indian sunset, his eyes wild with anger. Two girls sitting near the front of the class were shedding tears, and everyone was sitting upright, startled, waiting to see what would happen next. Young Freddy Mainwearing had been made to stand on his chair in front of the class (a mild punishment for Bassett!) and he sobbed fitfully, waiting to be flogged, as Bassett glowered at the class.

"Stop that snivelling, Main-Wearing!" Bassett yelled.

Well, I must admit that I completely lost my temper at that! In fact, to be perfectly honest, I resorted to physical violence – or tried to. My hand came up behind Bassett's ear with all the strength I could muster, then passed straight through his head! (I always knew that the man had little between his ears, but I had not suspected that it was *so* little!) It was, of course, the fact that I was dead.

How frustrating it was to swipe out at someone and miss! I tried again in the vain hope that this time it would work, but it did not. My hand sailed through Bassett's thick head and appeared not to affect him in the least. I glanced down at the cane which lay across the desk in a prominent position. If only I could hold that cane – if only I could grip it in my hand and – and—

As I thought about it, the cane slowly began to rise from the desk and sailed towards me! Gracious! Another Great Power had revealed itself!

I tried the same experiment with a piece of chalk, completely forgetting that the cane was now suspended in mid air. As my attention was diverted from the cane to the chalk, the cane fell to the floor with a loud clatter which made everyone, including Bassett, jump. He bent down, picked it up gently, then replaced it on the desk, evidently thinking that it had rolled to the floor by accident. Meanwhile, the chalk I was concentrating upon had floated up from the battered tobacco tin in which it was kept and was making its way towards me.

My next experiment was with a ruler which lay on the desk of young Andrew Smart. This was a most satisfactory experiment. Andrew noticed his ruler move, then, as it rose before his face he stood up, his eyes rounder than tea plates. "Look at that!" he yelled. "My ruler is floating!"

His reaction to my experiment attracted the attention of Mr Bassett, who was still glowering at the class. Naturally my concentration drifted, probably because I had not expected such a reaction, and the ruler fell to the desk with a loud report.

"Smart!" yelled Mr Bassett. "What are you doing, lad? Eh? Playing the fool again, are you?" Bassett now appeared to be extremely happy to have secured a victim without having to make up an excuse.

"It was my ruler, sir!" Andrew cried. "It just floated up from my desk!"

Bassett grinned, displaying his yellow teeth. This would be a "six of the best" case at least.

"Your ruler floated up off your desk?" Bassett asked.

"Yes, sir," said Andrew. "It just took off."

"Amazing," said Bassett. "I never cease to wonder

at the marvels of nature. One thing is for sure, Smart—"

"What's that, sir?" asked young Andrew innocently.

"That you were mis-named!" Bassett shouted. "Smart by name and stupid by nature," he went on. "If you think you can stand there, in my class, and make an exhibition of yourself without expecting punishment—"

"But it did!" Andrew replied.

"Ten of the best," said Bassett slowly. "Ten of the best, Smart, that's what you deserve."

"I saw it!" Andrew said. "Honest, sir!"

"That makes it fifteen," Bassett said evenly. "I can't abide liars."

Realizing that he was making matters worse, yet still exasperated by the unexplained incident, Andrew held his tongue. But Bassett now seemed intent on exacting revenge. "Have you anything to add to your statement?" he asked.

Fearing to utter even one word, Andrew blushed furiously.

"Dumb insolence!" Bassett screeched. "When I was in the army you could be put on a charge for that! Don't just stand there, boy – say something!"

As I had been the culprit in getting Andrew into such trouble, I decided that I ought to do my best to

help him. Using my newfound powers of concentration I managed to get the ruler to lift itself
from the desk.

"Look, sir!" Andrew cried. "It's doing it again!"

At first Bassett refused to look where the boy was
pointing. "You don't catch me out with childish
pranks like that," he said. "Twenty of the best, my
boy!"

With some difficulty I managed to steer the ruler
towards Bassett so that it hovered at his eye-level.
He stared at it, then blinked twice as if to remove the
image from his eyes. It was, of course, all a trick (he
thought).

"Make it go down," Bassett snarled. "I will not
have these cheap joke-shop tricks brought into my
classroom. We are here to study."

"I can't make it go down," Andrew said.

"You made it float," Bassett replied evenly. "Now
stop it from doing so before I increase your
punishment to thirty of the best."

"Thirty! I was astonished at the man's brutality.
How could he ever dream of caning a child thirty
times? It was disgusting.

But Bassett was now impatient to enjoy punishing
the boy. Too impatient to waste time. He lunged at
the floating ruler, but not before I had foreseen what
he was about to do. His hand grasped around fresh

air and he looked at his empty fingers in amazement. Thinking that young Andrew Smart was playing games with him, he cried out in anger, "Stop this nonsense, boy! Let me have that ruler!"

Again he lunged at the ruler, which I had whisked away from him so quickly. This time he succeeded in grasping it, and I concentrated my full energies so that it twisted out of his hand and floated up towards the ceiling. "Get that ruler down here, Smart!" he yelled. "I will not be made a fool of in front of the whole class!"

By this time I was enjoying my new powers enormously. So I obliged Mr Bassett by bringing the ruler down slowly, slowly, so that it came within inches of his outstretched hand. He reached up for it, standing on tip-toe, his fingers almost touching it. "More," he said. "Just a bit more and I can reach it—"

I teased him by holding the ruler just out of reach, then Bassett pulled a chair forward and stood on it. Imagine the fury on his face when I allowed the ruler to float up, just out of reach again!

"Andrew Smart!" he screamed. "Bring that ruler down!"

The children, although they did not understand how the ruler was managing to float by itself, were thoroughly enjoying the pantomime. Bassett was now making tiny leaps from the chair in an effort to reach the ruler, and I must admit that I did something rather naughty just as his feet left the seat of the wooden chair.

I made the chair move. Samantha Cooper screamed – but too late!

Now, Bassett knew as well as anyone that what goes up must come down again. He also thought that if he jumped *up* six inches, he would then *fall* six inches before reaching the chair once more. When he jumped up eight inches and fell twenty-four, the look of surprise on his face was wonderful to behold! It took a short space of time for him to fall to the floor, his arms and legs splayed out like those of a newborn lamb. He landed most untidily, his arms waving wildly in the air. Instantly he was on his feet, his right hand automatically reaching out for the cane. "You moved that chair!" he yelled at Andrew.

Rather than make matters worse, I decided that it was, indeed, time to bring the ruler down to Mr Bassett, and, if I may be permitted a moment of unashamed boastfulness, I think my aim was superb!

Mr Bassett is possessed of an enormous rounded bottom which appears to be straining continuously to tear his trousers asunder. His tailor, I hear, lives in mortal fear that his workmanship is perpetually on trial. When the ruler came sailing down and connected with that bottom, it gave out a very satisfactory report (far better than any report Bassett ever gave a child!), and the brutal teacher straightened up, his eyes bulging with the exquisite agony of it all.

"One!" I cried – although no one could hear me. Then I caused the ruler to strike again, but with more force this time. "Two!"

I had not expected Mr Bassett to possess the qualities of an athlete, but he demonstrated admirably that he was a superb high-jumper and could sprint respectably. His high-jump took him over the first desk, his feet just missing the head of young Alison Thomas.

"Three!" I followed him with the ruler, bringing it down with all the mental force under my control. Rather than leave matters to chance, I decided to devote some of my energies to lifting a stick of chalk from the tin on his desk so that I could keep count on the blackboard; but the children were too engrossed in the action to be aware of the phantom chalk steadily noting the punishment.

"Yipes!" screamed Bassett. "Wowee!" The ruler descended again and again as Bassett leaped and ran with remarkable agility. His mind was throwing out powerful thought waves as I made the ruler chase him, and I gathered that he was genuinely surprised at the fearfulness of the pain which the ruler was inflicting. But he was learning now, very quickly indeed!

"Twenty-eight, twenty-nine, thirty!" The ruler came down triumphantly, and Bassett, now too weak to run, lay exhausted over a chair (a position he had often demanded of pupils to be caned).

The chalk squeaked the last number on the board, and I resisted the temptation to give him one for luck, and made the ruler float slowly upwards until it touched the ceiling and stayed there as if by glue. Bassett looked up at it. He rubbed his eyes, unable to believe what he had experienced, and the children, equally dumbfounded, giggled aloud at him. Angrily he made to reach out for the nearest child, but I willed the ruler to float down threateningly in front of him and he withdrew his hands immediately, his eyes wide with fear.

Now that Bassett had learned to respect the hovering ruler, I decided to leave it up there, on the ceiling, where it would constantly remind him of his brutal ways. Willing a small tube of glue up to the ceiling was quite easy, but unscrewing the cap and squeezing a little out was more difficult to my unpractised mind. However, I managed it, and soon the ruler was stuck securely to the ceiling.

After all the excitement, I decided to have some fun. Firstly, I thought it would be wise for the children to be sent home so that they could recover from their experience. A couple of days' holiday would soon wipe the memory clear from their young minds.

Another thought which had been on my mind was to cause just a tiny bit of havoc in Mrs Simpkin's class. (The reason for this whim was that Mrs Simpkins is very well-ordered and precise, and I wanted to see what would happen if her cakes burned, or if her jellies refused to set!)

I floated down through the floor to the basement where the central-heating boiler gurgled and bubbled contentedly. Naturally I did not simply use my powers to turn the control knob to the 'Off' position, because someone would have noticed that almost immediately. What I did was to concentrate upon the thermostat so that the contacts bent away from each other at right-angles. It would, I knew, take quite some time to repair.

Whilst waiting for the temperature of the school to reach an uncomfortably cool degree, I amused myself by visiting the classes.

Mr Evans was most surprised, when he turned to face his blackboard, to see that he appeared to have written "The Battle of Hastings – 1966", and he hastily rubbed it out before the children could comment upon it. Mrs Simpkins was equally dumbfounded when a ring of the cooker kept switching itself on and off. In the chemistry laboratory I managed to make an evil-smelling gas which drove the pupils and the master into the playground, coughing and spluttering; and I finished my performance in the Integrated Studies class by making the globe of the world spin so fast that it fell from the table and whizzed around Mr Roper's feet like a spinning top!

By this time the temperature had dropped considerably, and Mr Bassett had adjourned to the staffroom for the next lesson. It was his free period, when he could mark exercise books and test papers.

Soon the headmaster was making his rounds to tell everyone that the central heating had broken down and that it would be wise for the children to go home. This, of course, delighted them.

As the head made his way towards the staffroom, I decided to play a trick on him which none of his pupils had so far dared to do. It was a simple matter to use my powers to raise a heavy mathematics book from the table behind Mr Bassett, and I carefully floated it around the walls of the room until it hovered over the staffroom door. When the headmaster opened the door, I was ready.

The book fell upon the round, bald patch with a resounding thudding noise, and Bassett looked up from his exercise books with a startled expression on his face.

"Mr Bassett!" roared the headmaster. "I am surprised at you!"

"Wha—?" Bassett was puzzled to see his headmaster sitting on the floor. "Did you fall?" he asked.

"I most certainly did not fall," came the reply. "If you must play childish tricks, kindly do so after school hours. Placing a book over the door is not a very intelligent thing for a teacher to do."

"But I didn't!" Bassett cried.

"Please do not compound matters by lying," the

headmaster said crossly. He stood up, rubbing the egg-shaped lump which was rising from his domed head. "You are the only person in the room, aren't you?"

Bassett agreed that this was so.

"And the book could not have been put up there before you came in, otherwise it would have fallen on your head."

The logic was faultless.

"And the book is yours," said the headmaster. "I think perhaps you had better see me in my study in the morning. We shall discuss your future at this school"

"My future?" Bassett asked.

"*If* you have a future here," came the retort.

Well, Mr Bassett did have a future with the school, and still has. You see, after the headmaster had left the room, Bassett went back to his work, shaking his head. He sat down, gazing dismally at the exercise book before him, then, as he was about to pick up his red pen, I caused it to move.

"Mighty mackerel!" Bassett cried, leaping from his chair. He watched, fascinated, as I made the pen skip and dance over the page of the exercise book, then, when I had finished writing, he cautiously picked up the book and began to read aloud.

"Dear Mr Bassett," he said, his voice becoming a

whisper as his eyes scanned the page. "I am sorry to have surprised you by writing in such a flamboyant manner, but I feel that your cruelty to the children deserves a comment from me. As you know, I have now passed on and I live beyond the restrictions of my old body. I shall be watching your behaviour very closely in the future, and you may rest assured that I will not hesitate to punish you should you raise your cane to the children ever again. I am sorry that this has to be such a severe letter, but I feel very strongly about all this. Yours sincerely, Ernest Morgan."

He stared at the page for some minutes, read the letter again, then suddenly grabbed at the page and shouted, "But this is fantastic! I have proof of life after death! Ghosts exist!"

And that is when I moved faster than I ever have done in all my death! I whisked the page from the book and floated it up, up, then out through the window (which, fortunately, was not quite closed), then on, across the playground towards the smoke of a bonfire which was crackling merrily at the bottom of the school garden.

Bassett watched the paper float away, then, without a word, he opened the cupboard door, selected an armful of canes and set off across the playground after the paper. When he reached the bonfire he threw the canes into the flames and stood there for some minutes, his face illuminated by the bright fire. It took two more journeys for him to dispose of all his stock, and when he had finished the task he returned to the staffroom, made himself a cup of tea and drank it thoughtfully.

Mr Bassett was a changed man.

I understand, from conversations I have overheard in the staffroom, that he went so far as to attend my funeral (something which even I could not bring myself to do, for I do so hate those miserable gatherings).

Of course, I expect you think this story is a complete fabrication, but I intend to prove to you that this is not the case. The name of the author at the beginning of the story should, of course, be Ernest Morgan, but I was forced to use this fellow, Tapp, to write it on his typewriter. I am certain that he would be quite upset if my name, and not his, appeared beneath the title, for the poor, deluded man is convinced that he has hit upon a brilliant idea in telling this story to you, and he has no notion that I am using his mind. Perhaps, sometime in the future, I may use him again!

Note from Editor to Printer:
Please delete the last paragraph from this story as I feel that it might frighten our readers if they suspect

that Ernest Morgan is still floating around. I have had permission to delete from the author, who swears he did not write it anyway!

Note from Ernest Morgan to the reader:

The printer did as he was told and did *not* make up the print for the last paragraph, so I had to spend all night in the printing works finding the right letters and laying it out neatly. I *told* you I have special powers, didn't I? Actually, I thoroughly enjoyed searching through all those boxes of printing letters to make this up, and I am happy to say that I have managed to do a good job, without a single misdake . . . I hope we meet again, soon!

You Can't Bring That in Here

Robert Swindells

Jimmy was absolutely fed up. His mum and dad had gone off to work in America for two years, leaving him to be looked after by his grown-up brother, Osbert. Looked after! That was a laugh, for a start. Osbert had worked in a bakery, but as soon as Mum and Dad started sending money from America, he chucked his job. Nowadays he spent most of his time lying on the sofa in his vest watching telly, slurping beer straight from the can and making rude noises. He neither washed nor shaved nor did anything around the house. The place smelled awful, and the sofa looked like a tatty boat afloat on a sea of can rings, beercans and screwed-up crisp packets.

Jimmy had to go to school, and when school was over he never had any fun. He couldn't bring his friends home because they were all scared of Osbert,

and if there was something good on telly his brother always said, "Shove off, kid – I'm watching *this*."

He made Jimmy do all the work – shopping, cooking, cleaning, ironing, gardening – in his spare time. On cold mornings Jimmy had to sit on the lavatory to warm the seat for Osbert, and at bedtime he had to lie in his brother's freezing bed till the sheets were warmed and Osbert came to kick him out. Soon his friends stopped bothering with him, because he couldn't play out or go to football. He grew lonely and sad.

One day on his way home from school, Jimmy found a baby bird which had fallen out of its nest. It was fluffy and cute and Jimmy felt sorry for it. "It's all right, little bird," he murmured. "I'm going to take you home and look after you."

But when he got home Osbert said, "You can't bring that in here."

"Why not?" asked Jimmy, dismayed.

"Birds make a mess," said Osbert, brushing crumbs off his vest. "Take it away. Get rid of it."

Jimmy sniffled as he walked along the street with the nestling cupped in his hands. How could he get rid of it? If he put it down, a cat would get it.

He met an old lady. "What have you got there?" she asked. Jimmy showed her. "Oh, the poor wee creature," she said. "And are you its new mammy?" Jimmy told the old lady about Osbert and she said, "I'll tell you what we'll do. I have a beautiful kitten at home. I'll swap you – your bird for my kitten."

Jimmy was sure Osbert would fall for the kitten, but he didn't. "You can't bring that in here," he said.

"Why not?" asked Jimmy.

"Kittens make a mess," said Osbert, throwing an empty can across the room. "Get it out."

Jimmy put the kitten in his pocket and went out. "Maybe I should take you back to the old lady," he whispered, but just then a boy from his school came along.

"Hi, Jimmy," he said. "What's that in your pocket?" Jimmy showed him the kitten and told him about Osbert. "I know," said the boy. "I'll take the kitten, and you can have my gerbil."

"You can't bring that in here," growled Osbert from the sofa. "Gerbils throw their food around."

"But – but—" stammered Jimmy.

"No buts!" roared Osbert, chucking half a pork pie at Jimmy's head. "Get it out of here."

Jimmy put the gerbil in his pocket and went out. It was getting dark and he was hungry. An old man was coming along the street with a puppy on a lead. "What's up, son?" he asked, because Jimmy was crying a bit. He told the old man about the gerbil, and about Osbert. "Well, here," said the old man. "Give me your gerbil and take my puppy. Nobody can resist a puppy."

Osbert could resist a puppy. "You can't bring that in here," he snarled. "Puppies wreck the place."

"Yes, but—" murmured Jimmy.

"No buts!" screamed Osbert, pounding the sofa with his fist till the arm fell off. "Get it out of here, and when you come back you can get my tea – I'm starving."

Jimmy was starving too, but he couldn't just abandon the puppy. He trailed along the street holding the lead, wondering what to do. I could try the RSPCA, he thought. They'd look after him. But when he got to the RSPCA it was shut. He was standing, looking at the CLOSED sign and wondering what to do, when a van drew up and a man got out. "Oh, heck," the man sighed. "Closed, and I thought I'd be getting rid of him at last."

"Who?" asked Jimmy.

"My pet," growled the man. "That's who."

"Why d'you want rid of him?" Jimmy asked.

"'Cause he's a gorilla," said the man.

"A gorilla?" Jimmy was amazed.

The man nodded. "Aye. Cute and cuddly he was, when he was small, but now . . ." He led Jimmy to the back of the van. "Look."

Jimmy peered through the window. Inside the van sat an enormous gorilla. "Wow!" he gasped. "What does he eat?"

"Bananas," said the man. "Loads and loads of bananas."

"And where does he sleep?"

"In my bed," said the man. "He kicked me out six months ago and now I have to make do with the floor."

"I'll swap you," offered Jimmy. "My puppy for your gorilla."

The man shook his head. "You don't want a gorilla, son," he said.

"Oh yes I do!" cried Jimmy.

Osbert was still on the sofa when Jimmy walked in,

his fist buried in the gorilla's giant paw. It was dark in the room and Osbert couldn't see his brother's new pet clearly. "You can't bring that in here," he said.

"He isn't bringing me," rumbled the gorilla. "I'm bringing *him*. And you can get off that sofa – it's mine."

Everything's changed at Jimmy's house now. The place sparkles, which isn't surprising because Osbert never stops cleaning it. He daren't stop, because Bozo the gorilla likes a tidy house, and Bozo usually gets what he wants. When Osbert isn't lugging great bagfuls of bananas from the

supermarket he's sweeping, polishing, dusting and hoovering. Jimmy's friends drop in all the time to watch TV, play video games and see Bozo. Until recently Osbert had a girlfriend, but she's left him now. She didn't like it when Osbert brought her home one evening and Bozo said, "You can't bring that in here."

Sticky Bun and the Sandwich Challenge

Janet Frances Smith

Hello. The name's Sam. Sam Bun. My friends call me Sticky. Sticky Bun. Gerrit? And they think it's dead funny that my dad runs a sandwich shop. Jaws, it's called. That's because Dad makes great whopping sandwiches full of cheese, or ham, or cheese and pickle, or ham and pickle, or cheese AND ham AND pickle.

Doorsteps my gran calls them. Docker's butties my mum calls them. You have to open your jaws really wide to bite one of my dad's sandwiches.

This story starts when Maxwell Morris made fun of my dad. Make fun of *me*, yeah. Make fun of my big sister Mollie, yeah. But my dad?

No chance.

Maxwell's a big lad. He can crush Coke cans with his head against the school wall. He's got a haircut as short as the grass on the bowling green and big, sticky-out ears like satellite dishes. I sometimes wonder when he talks to himself, if he's picking up Sky Sports or the Disney Channel and he can hear it in his head.

Maxwell Morris said, "Your dad couldn't make a sandwich to save his life."

"What?" I said.

"Your dad makes rotten sandwiches," said Maxwell.

We were sat at the packed lunch table in the school hall. In front of me was my old *Thomas the Tank Engine* sandwich-box from when I was in

Infants. I'd picked off most of the transfer so that the other kids didn't laugh at me. Mum can't afford to buy me a new one.

Maxwell's is a posh new football lunch-box, signed by some of the players at Man U. Or so he said. I think David Beckham's signature looks just like Maxwell's writing, but I'd be daft to say so. Do I want a squashed head? No, thank you.

Anyway, he was biting into a Mega Munch Energy Bar and you could almost see his muscles rippling, when he said this about my dad.

"What's wrong with my dad's sandwiches?" I said.

Maxwell looked at my lunch. If sandwiches could blush, then this one ought to have done. I know that. But I still couldn't have this dung-head slagging off my dad.

"*My* dad says the bread's dry, it's marge instead of butter and you need specs to see the filling," said Maxwell.

The other kids on the packed lunch table stopped eating and looked at me. The bit of sandwich still in my mouth began to taste like the insole of our Mollie's trainers.

Maxwell's ears twitched. He had probably tuned into another station. Snooker maybe.

"Your dad's sandwiches are boring."

From the corner of my eye I saw Sylvie Sanderson

look at me. She hated Maxwell more than any of us. Bag-of-spuds he calls her. Just because her dad runs the fruit and veg shop. And because she's a bit bigger than the other girls.

"Don't listen to him, Sticky," she said.

I felt the back of my neck start to go red. That was because of Sylvie. I felt my knees begin to wobble. That was because of Max. I cleared my throat and tried to deepen my voice.

"If we were in the playground," I said to Max, "I'd bash your head in." My deep voice must have got lost somewhere, because it came out in a squeak.

Maxwell laughed. You could see the huge gap where his front teeth had come out and there was spit and Mega Munch dripping in his mouth. It was like the cave of doom.

"*You* – bash *me*?" Maxwell bent his arms and did an impression of a Gladiator. He was right. Ever seen a stick insect? That's what I look like, except I'm not green.

"If your dad's so good at making sandwiches, why does he never have any customers?" sneered Maxwell.

"He does!" I said. But as the words came out I knew Maxwell was right. People came once. Twice maybe. But hardly ever again. That's why we didn't have much money at our house. Dad's sandwiches were boring. I should know. I had to eat them every day for my school dinner and the leftovers for my tea.

The noise of children in the hall sounded like the roar of a hundred railway engines in my ears. But through the sound I began to hear a voice. It was Sylvie. "You'll show him, won't you, Sticky?"

"Will I?!"

"You'll bring a great sandwich for your dinner tomorrow, won't you?"

"Will I?"

Then I looked across the table and saw her round face and pleading large blue eyes. And I found myself saying, "Yes. I'll show you, Maxwell Morris. You wait until tomorrow!"

Dad met me at the school gate when it was home time. He shut the shop early because there weren't any customers. It was the best time of the day for me. We'd play daft games on the way home. Dad would pretend we were from the Hole in the Wall Gang and that we had to get down the hill and past the chippy to our house without being spotted by the sheriff. That usually involved dodging in and out of people's doorways and we got some funny looks, I can tell you.

But I didn't feel like playing daft games. Dad tried. It was something to do with aeroplanes and going "Neeeiow!" down the street with our arms wide apart, but I didn't have the heart for it.

"What's up, son?" he said.

"Nothing, Dad," I said.

"When kids say 'nothing' it's usually 'something'," said Dad. He's clever like that. Not much gets past him. Except goals when he plays for the village team. But that's another story.

"Have you ever thought of making different sandwiches?" I said.

"Different?" He scratched the back of his head. "Sandwiches?"

"Yeah."

"You mean – not ham or cheese or pickle?"

"Yeah."

He needed time to think, to let the idea ooze into his brain. So I talked about the weather. He was looking at me as though my brains were cooked, but I still rattled on.

As luck would have it, Gran came for tea. Even my dad's face lit up when Gran came. It wasn't her as much as the shopping she always brought. "I'm not having stale sandwiches for my tea, our Pam," Gran said to my mother every Wednesday. "Got you a bit of shopping. Bit of nice bread. Some eggs. Lettuce."

We had a nice tea but Dad was unusually quiet.

"What's up with you?" Gran asked him.

"Different," Dad said and gazed into space.

205

I saw Gran later, checking the empty beer bottles. But I knew that Dad was thinking.

The next day, I was flying round, getting ready for school, when Dad gave me my lunch-box.

"Different," he said and winked. I didn't have time to say much, just grabbed it and ran. As it was, the bell had already gone before I sat down at my desk. At lunchtime, I suddenly remembered. Sylvie sat nearby and raised her eyebrows at me like you do when you're asking someone a question. I opened my lunch-box and there, inside, was a large foil-wrapped parcel. I was still staring at it when Maxwell blustered in and sat down opposite me.

"So – what have we got today, Sticky Bun?" he sneered at me.

"Probably the best sandwich in the world," I said.

Sylvie looked scared. I went hot then cold.

"Let's have a look then, dung-head," said Maxwell.

I peeled back the foil wrapping while my heart did a tap dance in my chest. And then I gasped.

Inside the foil were eight neat, triangular sandwiches – not the doorsteps I was used to. I picked one up and peered inside. It was cream cheese, dotted with chives, topped with finely shredded lettuce and thin slices of ruby red tomato. I forgot about Max. I even forgot about Sylvie. My mouth felt wet. I bit into one of the sandwiches. It was terrr-iffic!

"They look good," said Sylvie. "Can I have one?"

I passed one to her.

Maxwell said, "What are those funny green bits?"

"See, I told you," said Sylvie, munching my dad's sandwiches. "And I bet Sticky can bring a different sandwich every day next week."

I gulped.

"And the week after," she said.

I went hot and then cold.

"Hang on a bit," I mumbled.

But Maxwell had already begun to speak.

"OK then," he said. "Two weeks. I'll give him two weeks. And each sandwich has to be different and bigger and better than the rest. Or else."

"Or else what?" I squeaked.

He did his impression of a Gladiator and grinned. At least the gap in his front teeth grinned.

"Course he can do it," said Sylvie. "After all, his dad runs a sandwich shop."

Dad wanted to pretend to swim home when he collected me from school. "We can pretend that you're a shark and —"

"No, Dad, listen," I said. And then I told him. All about Maxwell and what he'd said about my dad and about the shop and about the sandwiches. Every-thing. Even about Sylvie.

"Don't worry, son," he said.

"But I am worried," I said. Thoughts of Dad's stale grey sandwiches flooded into my brain.

"I'll do the worrying," he said. "I'm a dad. That's what dads do."

So he went to the library on Saturday and brought home some cookery books. He started making lists, and when I wanted a kick-about at the park he wouldn't come. Later on, I suggested going out on our bikes, but he said he was going to the super-market. Weird.

Come Monday morning, I was flying round as usual, finding my reading book and stuffing my gym kit in my bag, when Dad came up to me, beaming all over his face. He had something behind his back.

Do you know what it was? It was an ace Man U lunch-box – bigger than Maxwell's.

"Good luck," said Dad and he winked.

Word had got round at school about the sandwich challenge. Loads of kids tried to cram on to my lunch table but Mrs Bones, the dinner lady, soon sorted them out.

But Maxwell managed to get near me. Sylvie was seven places away. My heart started bopping as the room went quiet. I opened my lunch-box. And there inside the foil parcel were turkey, tuna and tomato triangles oozing with salad cream. They looked terrific. They were terrific. Maxwell looked ticked off.

Tuesday came and when I opened my lunch-box, there were six double-decker pepperami, peanut butter and pickle sandwiches, with added pieces of pork pie.

By the end of the week – when I was tucking into cucumber, Camembert and coconut sandwiches, cut into the shape of footballs – even Mrs Bones began to take an interest.

"And what have we got today, Sam?" she asked me,

taking a peek. And when she saw them she said, "Think I'll have to take a walk down to your dad's shop this weekend if he can make sandwiches like that."

Max nearly choked on his Mega Munch.

The weekend didn't go down too well. Word had got round. People were queuing outside Dad's shop when he opened up on Saturday morning. Instead of being able to close early and come down to the park with me, he was still serving customers at tea time.

The shop was shut on Sunday, but Dad hadn't got time for me then. He was either out shopping for some special ingredients or poring over cookery books.

I'd got one more week to do.

On Monday I had spicy sausage, soya sauce, sardine and sago sandwiches. On Tuesday I had cheese, chutney, chocolate and chive sandwiches. On Wednesday I had carrot, cress, cottage cheese and crisp sandwiches. On Thursday I had banana, bacon and blancmange sandwiches. And on Friday I had triple-decker chocolate chip, jam and jelly sandwiches.

And on Saturday – I was sick. My tummy ached, my head hurt and my legs felt like jelly. I never wanted to see another sandwich in my life.

Mum looked after me. Dad was too busy coping

with the queues in the shop. Sylvie came to see me. She ate the grapes she'd brought me and told me Maxwell had stopped calling her names.

A reporter from the local newspaper came and told Dad he was in the running for the Super Sandwich award. A photographer took a picture of him, biting into one of his famous Cherry Chomper sandwiches.

When I felt a bit better on Saturday afternoon, I was watching the queue from my bedroom window. I nearly fell through the glass when I saw Maxwell's dad there.

But it was all getting a bit too much. Dad was flaked out on Sunday. "Exhausted, I am," he said.

"Come to the park, Dad?"

"Sorry, son – and I won't be able to pick you up from school tomorrow. Shop's too busy."

"Oh," I said.

"What's the matter, son?" he said.

"Nothing."

"When a kid says 'nothing' he means 'something'," said Dad. "What's wrong?" We talked then, me and Dad. Talked until tea time. And by then I was feeling well enough to try one of Dad's spicy sausage sandwiches. Nice it was, too. The next day, there in my lunch-box was a foil-wrapped parcel. The other kids crowded round. For once Mrs Bones didn't stop them. But when I peeled back the foil they all gasped.

211

Staring me in the face was a rather ordinary, boring cheese sandwich. Maxwell didn't say a word. Sylvie winked at me. And when school finished, there was Dad waiting for me at the gate, wearing a black patch over his eye.

"Pirates tonight, Dad, right?" I said. And we swashbuckled our way home, past the chippy, aboard our pretend galleon.

We popped into the shop before we went down to the park for the kick-about. Sylvie's mum was there in a bright green overall, laughing with the customers. And Maxwell's mum was behind the counter too. Both of them were serving the never-ending queue.

Dad reckons, as he was the brains behind the whole thing, he deserves a break. So he leaves Sylvie and Maxwell's mums in charge at tea time and picks me up from school. Sylvie drops by most days, too. She joins me and Dad in the park. She's a great goalie.

And me? Oh, I have school dinners now.

Mystery Tour

Jan Mark

"**D**o you want the good news first, or the bad news?" says Fig, on the telephone. And then, before I can answer, goes on, "or the worse news, or the very worst?"

"The bad," I said, and added quickly, "then the good," because if I let Fig run on to the worse news and then the worst, I might not be in any condition to enjoy the good news.

"OK," Fig said, sounding just like the man at the station who cancels trains. "Mum can't take us to London next week. She's got an interview."

"Oh," I said. I felt as though I'd known that would happen all along. After *my* mum refused to let me go to London with Fig alone and unsupervised – those were the words she used – it seemed too good to be true when Fig's mum said that she would take us. I'd been right. It was too good to be true.

"What's the good news, then?"

"My Auntie Cathy will take us instead."

I'd seen Fig's Auntie Cathy once or twice. "That's the *good* news?"

"It's better than not going at all," Fig said. "I think."

"What's the worse news?"

"She can't drive. We're going by coach."

"That's not the end of the world."

"And she's bringing Damian too."

"That's the end of the world." Damian is Fig's cousin. He is four years old. He whines for England.

"Can't she get a babysitter?"

"She says it's time Damian went to London."

"Why? What's London done?"

Fig and I had planned to go to London to visit the Science Museum. Fig's mum had said that was fine by her, she'd go to the V & A next door and meet us afterwards. Auntie Cathy, as it turned out, had other ideas.

"She says it's a pity to go all that way just for one museum," Fig reported, next morning. "She says we ought to go early and make a proper day of it."

"Doing what?"

"Dunno," Fig said, gloomily. "She's got something lined up. She says we'll find out when we get there."

"Magical mystery tour?"

"Tragical history tour," Fig said.

Mum got me up at *six* on Friday morning, so I could leave at seven-fifteen to meet Fig and Auntie Cathy and Damian at the bus stop in time to catch the seven-forty coach. As I came round the corner into the main road I saw them standing in a row at the end of the queue and it was clear, from the way they were standing, that there had already been a row of some sort.

When they saw me coming Fig switched on a heavy scowl as an early warning, but Auntie Cathy whipped a shiny smile into place. Damian, who looked like a dwarf Sumo wrestler in green Bermuda shorts, was head-butting a nearby litter bin.

"You must be Ozzie," says Auntie Cathy, which made me want to say why must I be? But before I got the chance the coach drew up and Auntie Cathy, who had seemed daft but steady up to that point, if you see what I mean, began flapping. She's the sort of woman who looks as though she's been put together out of string. Everything she wore had loops and knots and fringes on it. Even her hair looked like that fuzzy tuft you get on macramé plant-pot holders. When she flapped, all the loose ends flapped too.

"Oh my goodness, you cut that fine, didn't you, we might have missed it, oh—"

"It's early," Fig growled. "Anyway, they go every twenty minutes."

"I think it's the seven-twenty running late, actually," I said. I don't like bossy grown-ups, but I *can't stand* bossy grown-ups who know less than I do. They make me go stiff and grind my teeth. I had a timetable too, and she didn't. And now she was wound up she began to spin. She had an enormous string tote-bag hung on her shoulder and she was scrabbling about in it, up to the elbows, like churning. Things started coming to the top – tissues, apples, books, freezer boxes, bottles. The queue was moving away from us. Fig managed to steer her towards the door of the coach by walking forwards until she had to step backwards, but by the time we were at the head of the queue she was still head-first in the tote-bag.

"You haven't lost your purse again, have you?" Fig

hopped on to the coach and hung out of the doorway in case the driver got fed up and left without us. All along the side of the coach you could see irritated faces pressed against the windows, wondering what the hold-up was. They weren't any more irritated than me, I can tell you.

"It's in here somewhere," Auntie was blathering.

"I want to go home." That was Damian. "I don't like queues. I want to watch television." He started kicking the coach.

"I've got a fiver," said Fig, getting desperate. "What about you, Oz?"

"So've I." I waved the note urgently under Auntie Cathy's nose. "Ten pounds'll pay for one and two halves. Under-fives are free."

"Are you thinking of coming with us?" the driver asked. Inside the coach the other passengers were starting to mutter. People use these early coaches to get to work on. They don't think much of day-trippers, especially batty day-trippers. Someone said, "Ever travelled by coach before, lady?"

"I'll go to a cash-till when we get to London," Auntie promised. "I'll pay you back then. I've got my purse in here somewhere, but – Oh, one and two halves, please, driver, *so* sorry – I put the money for the fares on the hall tables, so as to remember it on the way out – no, that one's under five ..."

The coach was full and we could not sit together – fortunately. Fig and I were one behind the other at the back and Auntie Cathy was in the middle, with Damian on her lap; near enough, though, for us to be able to hear Damian.

"I want to sit by the window. Why can't I sit by the window? I want to go home. I feel sick. I want to go to the toilet. *Why* can't I sit next to the window? I want to watch television." In the end it just became a sort of high-pitched noise in the background: "Iyiyiyiyiyiyiyiyyyyyyyyy . . ."

"Does he go on like that all the time?" I asked Fig. I had to lean forwards and sideways because Fig was in the seat ahead of me.

"Yes, but can you blame him?" Fig said, over his shoulder. "He didn't want to come, anyway. And she's turned the whole day upside down because of him."

I was alarmed. "Why? Aren't we going to the Science Museum, then?"

"Yes, but we're going somewhere else as well, first."

"Where?"

"She won't tell me. It's supposed to be a lovely surprise."

"I hate surprises," I said. "I like to know what's going on." And without the five pounds I felt unprotected. So long as you've got money with you,

you feel there's a way out. Without it you feel trapped, you're at other people's mercy. Grown-ups never seem to realize that, though you'd think they'd feel it more than we do.

"Well, we're having a picnic somewhere, if it doesn't rain. That was meant to be a secret too, but Damian was digging around in the bag and found the sandwich boxes."

Damian's voice rose up to new heights. "I don't want to go to London. I don't want to sit on your lap. I want to look out of the window."

"If it goes any higher," I said hopefully, "we won't be able to hear him at all. Like a bat."

We waited for that to happen, but it didn't, so we spent the rest of the journey working out ways to lose Damian in London. Most of them were quite cruel, involving escalators and live rails, but we couldn't plan anything in detail because we didn't know where we were going. I don't really mind surprises, so long as I don't know they're going to happen until they do happen, if you see what I mean. What I can't stand are surprises that you are expecting, the kind that you can see creeping up on you, like this one. Because with Auntie Cathy's kind of surprise you have plenty of time to imagine what it might turn out to be, and to be afraid that it will be a dis-appointment when it does happen. Or a disaster. Fig and I were fairly sure that we wouldn't enjoy anything that Auntie Cathy might spring on us.

Also, we didn't have a lot of faith in Auntie Cathy at all, what with her bringing Damian and *not* bringing enough money. Fig said he thought the best thing of all would be losing both of them.

"But not till she's been to the bank," I said. "When we've got our money back, we'll lose them."

We were joking, of course.

And we didn't get our money back.

When the coach got to Baker Street, *really* into the traffic jams, Fig waded up the aisle to ask Auntie Cathy where we'd be getting off. When he came back he didn't look too pleased.

"Don't tell me," I said. "It's a surprise."

"No – she says we'll go on to Victoria Station if the traffic's clear down Park Lane, but if it isn't we'll get off at Marble Arch. She says she knows an alternative route. She's got the tube map out."

"At least she's got a map," I said. "You can't go wrong with the tube map. It's got names on. It isn't just X marks the spot."

"Look here," Fig said, bitterly, "she got lost coming to the bus stop. *That* was an alternative route. We only got there a couple of minutes before you did."

"And then she complained that *I* was late," I said. I saw then that if anything did go wrong today, it would be our fault, even if we didn't lose Auntie Cathy or push Damian under a train.

Things started to go wrong at Marble Arch. OK, blame the traffic. If we'd gone on to Victoria *none* of it would have happened, but it took twenty minutes to get from Baker Street to Marble Arch – on the coach. You can walk it in ten. And so we all piled out. This time Damian wanted to stay *on* the coach because he could see that now there were lots of empty seats next to windows, but Fig kind of lifted him down the steps on the toe of his trainer – no, it wasn't a kick – without Auntie Cathy seeing and we headed back up the road to the tube station.

"Hang about," said Fig, running on ahead to the corner, "I can see a bank – hint, hint," so we went down Oxford Street to the bank, which was quite a long way down, but when we got there it was shut because it wasn't nine-thirty yet. Auntie Cathy zoomed towards the hole in the wall, waving her cash card. Out came some money – after she'd punched in the wrong number and then asked for a new cheque book instead of cash.

What we didn't realize, until it was too late, was that the hole in the wall only had twenty-pound notes in it, so Fig and I didn't get our fivers back.

"Don't worry, I'll get change at the station," Auntie Cathy trilled, so we trekked back to Marble

Arch and down the steps to the underground.

More trouble; Damian didn't like it. Well, I didn't like it myself. Marble Arch underground station can't be anybody's favourite place, but I didn't go blue in the face and start screaming, even when Auntie still didn't give us our dosh, though I felt like it. He didn't like the crowds and he didn't like the queue at the ticket window, but what he didn't like most of all was a sort of eerie yoo-hooing that came yodelling up the escalator and, really, it was a bit like something out of *An American Werewolf in London*, but we did think he might stop when we explained that it was only a busker. He didn't. It turned out he didn't know what a busker was and by the time we got to the bottom of the escalator he was practically trying to climb back up it again. Still, at least he could see it was only a hairy dude with a guitar, singing "On Blue Bayou".

We still hadn't got our money back, though.

At least we had our tickets. Auntie had had to give us those to get through the automatic gates. Hooray for automatic gates. If it hadn't been for the tickets we might still be going round and round.

You turn right at the bottom of the escalator at Marble Arch, and there is a staircase down to the lines, which run east and west, with a passage between the platforms. We could hear a train roaring

down there and a terrific draught came up that set all of Auntie Cathy's fringes flapping. We were halfway down the stairs while she was still peeling Damian off the escalator and dragging him past the werewolf, so by the time she caught us up the train had gone.

"Was it east-bound or west-bound?" Auntie said.

"West."

Fig was scowling again but Auntie Cathy gave a light laugh.

"Not to worry. We'll get an east-bound train instead."

"Change of plan?" I said, innocently, but she wasn't falling for that.

"Never you mind. We'll get there soon enough."

That started Damian off again. "*Where* are we going? Are we lost? I don't like it here. I want to go to the toilet."

There was an east-bound train due in two minutes, which gave Auntie Cathy time to nip along the platform and check out the big tube map on the wall. We scooted after her to see if we could guess what she was up to, but she just did squiggly movements with one finger, like the map was in Braille, that took in half a dozen stations. She could have been pointing at anywhere.

"Oh, that's fine," she said. "We'll change at Bond Street, on to the Jubilee Line, and then change again—"

"What's a jublyline? I don't want a jublyline," Damian said. "I want to go to the park."

"We *are* going to the park – well, it's a sort of park," Auntie said, cautiously. "Oh, look, here's the train."

It was packed, that train. It was like those pictures you see of the Tokyo underground where they've got people specially employed to push the passengers on board until the doors shut. Only we had to get ourselves on, and we were all squashed together in one corner, up against the fire extinguisher. Damian was starting to go purple, with rage or oxygen starvation.

"I want to go to the park. I want to see ducks."

"We'll see ducks, darling."

"I want to see aeroplanes."

"I expect we'll see aeroplanes. Yes, I'm sure we will."

Fig leaned over and said, man to man – well, man to auntie – "Look, where *are* we going, exactly?"

"Ask no questions and I'll tell you no lies," Auntie Cathy twittered.

"We are going to the museum, aren't we?" I said, trying to look tearful. I nearly was, too. With fury.

"Of course we are – *afterwards*. Here we are. Out we get. All stick together!" she made everything sound like PE at first school.

Half the passengers seemed to get out at Bond Street and we were swept along the platform towards the sign that pointed to the Jubilee Line. It was all we could do to stick together, but you could always tell where Damian was. I had him in my earhole all the way. "Where's the park? Where's the ducks? Where's the aeroplanes?"

Then we got sucked into a whirlpool of people at the bottom of the escalator and suddenly, as we shot out on to the platform, Damian's voice was coming from up ahead.

"I don't want to go on another train. I want to see the aeroplanes. *Where* are we going?"

"Oh, be quiet!"

225

I looked round at Fig. He raised his eyebrows. Even Auntie Cathy had had enough.

The Jubilee Line platform was emptier; there were only about a hundred people on it instead of five thousand, and there was room to breathe. It was the south-bound platform, so I suppose most people were heading the other way, for the middle of London. Fig and I went straight to the wall map to see if we could guess where we were going, when Damian let rip again.

"Where are we going? I don't like this. Where are we going?"

"Wait and see," Auntie Cathy said, but she was weakening, I could tell, and Damian could tell, too. He knew just how to handle her. Fig and I had been too restrained.

"Where are we *going*?"

Suddenly Auntie Cathy's fringes started floating again and I heard the train approaching. And I also heard her say, "Oh, for heaven's sake! First of all we're going to queue for the picnic—"

"I don't want to queue," Damian howled. "I want to go to the park. Why—"

And then the train roared in. I'm not sure what happened next, but Auntie Cathy and Damian were nearer to the edge of the platform than we were. This train was packed too, and as the doors opened a great mob of people surged out, and Damian and Auntie Cathy disappeared. Fig and I fought our way towards the nearest door, but just as we were about to get on, some more idiots who'd been stuck in the middle of the carriage came thundering out and we got swept back again, and before we could do anything the doors had shut and the train had started.

We just stood there. People were barging round us and shoving, and then there was no one, just us, and the last carriage of the train sliding past, towards the tunnel. And we'd both seen the same thing – Auntie Cathy hadn't noticed. When the doors closed she was still squawking at Damian who was still squawking at her. I turned to Fig.

"What shall we do?"

"How should I know?"

"I mean, will she come back for us or will she wait for us to catch up?"

"How can we catch up? We don't know where she's going."

"She said we'd have to change again."

"I know, but she didn't say where."

"She started to tell Damian, something about queuing for a picnic, but I didn't hear all of it." If only he'd worn her down faster!

I tried to stay calm. Ever since I was tiny and started going places with Mum, she's always said the same thing: "If we get separated, stay put. I'll come back for you." I somehow didn't think that Auntie Cathy would do anything that sensible.

"She's bound to notice in a minute," Fig said. "We'd better stay here."

So we sat down on those funny little seats that stick out of the wall like plastic laps. Another train came in. I looked at my watch: ten minutes. Then Fig said, "She'll be on the other line, won't she? This is the south-bound. North-bound's across the hall."

"But she'll know we're here, won't she?"

"Why hasn't she come back, then? She must be waiting for us."

"*Where*?"

But, just in case, we crossed the hall to the north-bound platform and went to study the wall map while we waited. "Look," Fig said, "there's only two places where you can change on the Jubilee, south of here: Green Park and Charing Cross. It doesn't go any further than Charing Cross."

"So where were we supposed to be going when we did change?" That was the trouble, there were so many lines. At Green Park you can change on to the Piccadilly and the Victoria. Charing Cross is for the Northern and the Bakerloo.

"Maybe it was Green Park," Fig said. "She did say it was a sort of park we were going to."

"Green Park's a real park," I said, "not a sort of anything. And we were going to change, not get out."

"She said there'd be aeroplanes. Where would we go to see aeroplanes?"

I was looking at my watch again: twenty minutes, now. I was starting to get really worried. Surely the silly bat had realized that we didn't know where she was and would come back for us. Then it struck me that since we'd crossed to the north-bound platform, there hadn't been any trains for her to come back *on*, and at the same moment there was a kind of booming explosion overhead and a voice said, "Good morning, ladies and gentlemen; this is your Jubilee Line information service. Owing to a defective train at Green Park, all services on this line will be subject to delay and cancellation." And then there was a lot more about going round by Oxford Circus to Baker Street. So that was why Auntie Cathy hadn't come back; the line was blocked.

"We'll have to go after her," I said.

"Yes, but *where*?" We seemed to take turns to say this.

"If she's not at Green Park she'll be at Charing Cross." I tried to sound confident.

"Yes, but supposing she knows about the defective train? Maybe *she's* coming back via Oxford Circus."

"Maybe she's on the defective train."

We were beginning to realize what a mess we were in, because in losing Auntie Cathy we'd lost everything else: coach tickets, money, food . . . all we had were our underground tickets. We were all right so long as we stayed underground. We'd checked them right away to see if they had the destination on, but it only said where we'd come from, Marble Arch, and they were singles, so as soon as we went through a barrier we'd be stuck, penniless, somewhere in London. And neither of us knows London well – that's the trouble with the tube map. It makes you think you know where you are, only London isn't the same shape as the map.

"Let's go to Green Park," Fig said. "Even if she did get as far as Charing Cross before she missed us, she'd have got as far as Green Park coming back." So we nipped across the hall again and there was a south-bound train coming in. It wasn't so crowded as the other one but we didn't sit down. We stood by the doors and peered out as if we might see Auntie Cathy and Damian slogging back through the tunnel, but all we did see were those strange pipes that wiggle along the tunnel walls, and when we got to Green Park – they weren't there, either.

It was getting serious. We were trapped.

"Haven't you got *any* money?" I asked Fig. He looked in all his pockets.

"Ten p. We could ring home."

"When will your mum be in? Mine's out till five."

"Six," Fig said. "She had to go to Birmingham – for that interview."

We tried to decide which would be worse: pounding the streets of London all day or lurking in the bowels of the earth.

"Let's find a map again and try to work this out," I said.

We found another map, with about fifteen gibbering tourists round it, but at last they cleared off and we closed in.

"Right," Fig said, "aeroplanes. Where are there aeroplanes?"

"Hendon," I said, "the aircraft museum." After a long search we found Hendon, up near the top of the Northern Line.

"Couldn't be Hendon, then," Fig said, "otherwise we'd have gone north at Bond Street."

"Maybe she was going to get the Northern Line at Charing Cross."

"But it would have been easier to stay on the Central and change at Tottenham Court Road – and quicker."

"What about the Imperial War Museum, then – that's got aeroplanes."

"Where do we get out for that?"

"Lambeth – that's on the Bakerloo. There you are, we'd have changed at Charing Cross."

"No, it'd be quicker to stay on the Central till Oxford Circus," Fig said. "What about Docklands? That's got an airport."

"It's not on the underground, though," I said. "It's got its own railway."

"Where?"

"I don't know," I snapped. "Docklands is the East End, isn't it?"

"Hang about," Fig said, "they're *all* in the east, aren't they?"

"Hendon's not," I said.

"East*ish*. Easter than Marble Arch. Don't you

remember, when we got down the escalator at Marble Arch we were after a west-bound train and we missed it?"

I did remember. "That's right, and she said it didn't matter because we could get an east-bound and change at Bond Street. But we were *heading* west, we were meant to be."

And we both looked at the left-hand edge of the map, and there, right at the end of the Piccadilly Line, where it turns back on itself, was a little picture of an aircraft, and we both said, at the same moment, "Heathrow!"

"Do you really think she'd take us all the way out to Heathrow?"

"We're on the Piccadilly Line here," Fig said.

"It's a hell of a way," I said. "Suppose we go all the way out there and we've made a mistake?"

"How much does it cost? Suppose we get out there and we've got the wrong tickets?"

I was still clutching my ticket and it was getting damp. I squinted at it again, in the hope that I might have missed something important the first time, but all it said was MARBLE ARCH C SINGLE 60, the date and lots of numbers.

"What's the C stand for?" Fig said.

"Child, I expect."

"And the 60?"

"Sixty pence?"

"Look," Fig said, "they're singles. How were we meant to get back?"

"By air?" I said, but Fig was past smiling.

"How *can* we get back?"

"Just hang on to the tickets," I said. "We're safe so long as we don't go through a barrier. We'll go to Heathrow, and if she's not there we'll come back here."

"But it'll take so long," Fig wailed, "and there's two stations at Heathrow."

"Let's start, anyway," I said. "You're right, it'll take ages. Maybe we'll have a better idea before we get there."

We were just moving off to find the Piccadilly Line when Fig said, "What's that?"

"What's what?"

"That other map."

I hadn't noticed the other map, but it was on the wall next to the one we'd been looking at. All the tube lines were on it, but it was in patches of different colours, like contours: blue in the middle, then out through yellow, orange and so on. "Zones", it said. Five of them.

Heathrow was in Zone Five.

I looked at the ticket again: 60p. We'd never get to Heathrow for 60p.

"Hendon's in Zone Three," I said. "Well, it's on the border."

"But we weren't going north. What about Lambeth?"

"Zone One. We wouldn't have needed a 60p ticket for Zone One. Anyway, we weren't going east."

Fig moaned and banged his head on the map. No one took any notice. No one had taken any notice of us at all. You wouldn't think you could feel so alone among so many people.

"Oz," Fig pleaded, "think again. Try and remember exactly what Auntie Cathy told Damian about what we were going to do."

"I told you, I only heard a bit of it. She said we'd have to queue for the picnic first of all."

"I don't get it," Fig said. "Why would we have to queue? She had the picnic in the bag."

"Perhaps it was a special place where you had to queue to get in."

"Oh, come off it," Fig said. "You can picnic free all over London. There's the parks . . . and the river . . ."

"The river!" I said. "Maybe we were going to come back by river. And look, if we were by the river we'd see the planes going into Heathrow."

"Heathrow's in Zone Five."

"Yes, but the Thames isn't. The Thames is in Two and Three, mostly. One even."

We looked at the map again, and then Fig jumped, and grabbed my arm.

"*What* did she say?"

"When?"

"About the picnic."

"That we'd be queuing for it."

"Are you sure? Think. What did she say exactly?"

"I can't remember. Something like, 'First of all we'll have to queue for the picnic' – no – 'We're *going* to queue for—'"

Fig was grinning and stabbing at the map with his finger, near the river, at a station like Hendon, right on the edge of Zone Three: Kew Gardens.

"You dork!" Fig yelled. "That's what she meant. We're going to Kew for the picnic – there you are. Kew. K-E-W. We can go on Victoria and change to the District Line, or we can get the Piccadilly Line here and change at Earl's Court."

We went via Victoria and got on a train to Richmond. Kew Gardens was the last station but one. It took us exactly twenty-nine and a half minutes, which was less time than we'd spent hanging around between Bond Street and Green Park, but it felt like hours, because we weren't sure, up to the last minute, if we were right, and even if we were, it didn't mean that Auntie Cathy would be there, but she was. After Earl's Court the line's above ground, just like an ordinary railway, and there on the platform was Auntie Cathy, and Damian. Damian was crying and Auntie Cathy looked as if she had been. Even her fringes were all damp and droopy. When she saw us she leapt up and *hugged* Fig, and he didn't even struggle.

I thought we'd get a rocket, but even that didn't happen.

"It's all my fault," Auntie Cathy kept saying, and I thought of asking for that in writing, but she really was crying now, with relief. "I *ought* to have told you. I just kept praying that you'd overheard me telling Damian."

"It's OK," Fig said, patting her on the back, "but we thought you'd come back for us."

"I did," Auntie Cathy sniffed, "but the train got stuck so I came round by Oxford Circus and by the time I'd got back to Bond Street, you'd gone. How did you guess where we'd be?"

"Deduction," Fig said, grandly. "We worked it out by a process of elimination."

He didn't let on that I'd half overheard her telling Damian where we were going, because that would have spoiled the effect. In fact it would have made us look as daft as she is, but Fig is a true friend and he didn't drop me in it. He didn't drop Auntie in it either, when we got home. The whole thing is a horrid secret and I have changed names to protect the guilty.

The Horrible Story

Margaret Mahy

Outside it was quite dark, but inside the boys had a candle-lantern which cast a pale, flickering light on the tawny sides of the tent. You could not see much – only the long shapes of sleeping-bags and blankets, and the humpy shapes of heads and pillows.

The two longest shapes were Robert and Allan, who were by the door flap, which was fastened back tonight. They had told Christopher, Robert's little brother, that they wanted to look out into the garden and watch the stars, but really they had their own secret reasons for wanting to be together by the door, and for making him sleep on his own at the back of the tent. *His* bedtime shape was just blankets, for he had no sleeping-bag, and it was a shorter shape than Allan's or Robert's, because he was only small – not quite seven – and they were ten.

Yesterday morning there had been no tent. A large

parcel had arrived at lunch time addressed to Mr Robert and Mr Christopher Johnson. Robert's eyes had shone with surprise and delight when it had been opened, and its layers of paper and cardboard peeled back. It was a tent – not just a white tent such as you might see in any camp-ground either, but a tawny-brown tent that could belong to an Indian or an outlaw or some wild, fierce hero.

There had been the fun of fitting the poles together and putting it up at the bottom of the garden, sheltered by the hedge, and the sudden excitement when they realized that they would be allowed to sleep out all night in it.

"Can Allan come too, Mum?" asked Robert, because Allan was his best friend, and they always shared adventures.

"Of course he may, if he is allowed," Mother replied, smiling.

"Me too!" Christopher cried anxiously, for he knew that when Allan and Robert were together he was always just a little brother to be left behind or taken no notice of. "It's *my* tent too, isn't it?"

Robert looked at him rather sourly. He said, "You can come some other time. You've got lots of chances."

His mother turned round sharply.

"Now, don't be difficult, Bob!" she said. "Of course

Christopher can camp out too. If there's no room for Christopher there's no room for Allan either."

So here they were, the three of them, Allan and Robert, and Christopher on his own in the back of the tent, looking a bit lonely and small in the flickering shadows.

Secretly Allan nudged Robert as a sign that he was going to begin the Get-rid-of-Christopher plan . . . a plan they had made that afternoon riding their bicycles home from the river.

"Little kids get scared easy as easy in the dark," Allan had said, his wet, red hair standing on end, his green eyes narrowed against the wind. He had glanced behind to see if Christopher was listening. The little boy had had his usual dreamy look and was practising his whistling. "I bet when your little brother hears one of my famous horrible tales he'll run inside to Mummy and won't want to come into the tent ever again. Then we'll have a midnight feast, eh? I'll bring a tin of fruit salad, and a tin opener, and some luncheon sausage."

"I'll buy a packet of biscuits," Robert had replied. "I've got ten pence."

As he remembered this he slid his hand under the pillow to feel the biscuits he'd hidden there. The paper crackled, and Christopher turned his head a little bit. Quickly Robert nudged Allan to show that he understood the plan was beginning. Allan blew out the candle in the lantern and for a moment everything went black as the night came, silent and sudden, into the tent.

"Hey," said Allan, "I know a story. It's pretty ghostly though . . ." He let his voice fade away uncertainly.

"Go on!" Robert said. "Tell us! I'm not scared."

"I'm not scared either," said Christopher's piping voice from the back of the tent. He did not sound the least bit like a wild, fierce hero though.

"It's good you're not scared," Allan declared, "because it's a really horrible story, and it's about a boy called Christopher too. Now listen!

"This boy called Christopher lived in an old, dark house on the edge of a big forest. The forest was old too, and dark, like this tent, and full of creepy noises. Sometimes people went in, but no one ever came out again. Lots of rats lived in this forest, big as cats . . ." Allan paused, thinking out the next bit. In the little silence Robert was amazed to hear Christopher's small voice come in unexpectedly.

"When those rats ran around," he said, "their feet made a rustly sound, didn't they?" Outside, the hedge rustled in the wind, and Christopher added, ". . . a bit like that."

"Huh!" said Allan crossly. "And I suppose you

think you know what else lived in the forest?"

"Yes . . . yes, I do, Allan."

"Look, who's telling this story?" cried Allan indignantly. Then he asked rather cautiously, "Well, what else *did* live there?"

"Spiders," said Christopher. "Big hairy spiders . . . big as footballs . . . but hairy all over like dish mops, huge black dish mops going scuttle, scuttle on lots of thin legs—"

Allan interrupted him fiercely, "Hey shut *up*, will you! This is my story, isn't it? Well then . . . there weren't any spiders, but there was a dragon."

Allan went on talking about the bigness and smokiness of the dragon, but Robert felt disappointed in it. Somehow it did not seem nearly as frightening as the scuttling, hairy spiders. On the other side of the tent something went *tap, tap, tap!* like quick little feet running over the canvas. Allan stopped and listened.

"It's just the wind," Christopher said in a kind voice. "It's just a scraping, twiggy piece from the hedge. Go on, Allan."

Robert suddenly felt sorry for Christopher, lying there so trustingly staring into the dark with round black eyes like shoe buttons. Christopher was just not an adventurer. He was not the sort of boy who knew anything about the wild scaring life of the wide world. Christopher was the sort who would rather stay at home and read fairy stories than plan wars in the gorse or battles over the sand hills. Perhaps it was a bit mean to frighten him out of the tent, a tent which was really half his.

"Never mind!" thought Robert. "He'll have lots of other chances." Under his pillow the biscuit paper crackled faintly.

"And then, one night . . ." Allan said mysteriously, "the little boy was on his own in the old house when . . . guess what happened?"

"Somebody knocked at the door," said Christopher promptly. "Three knocks, very slowly, KNOCK KNOCK KNOCK, like that."

"Fair go!" replied Allan scornfully. "Do you know who it was, Mr Smart?"

"Yes," Christopher went on, "the little boy opened the door and there was a man there all in black, at least it looked like a man, but you couldn't tell really, because he had a black thing over his face, a black silk scarf thing. And do you know what he said? He said, 'Little boy, the time has come for you to follow *me*.'" Christopher stopped, and the tent was quiet except for the sad-sea sound of the wind.

"Did the boy go?" asked Robert. He did not want to ask, but suddenly he felt he had to know. Allan said nothing. Christopher's voice was almost dreamy, as he replied,

"Yes, he did. He just couldn't help it. And as he went out of the door it shut itself behind him. The gate did too. Then they were in that forest. Everywhere was the rustling noise of rats and spiders."

"Hey—" began Allan.

"What?" squeaked Christopher. Allan turned over restlessly in the dark.

"Nothing! Go on!" he said.

"And *things* followed them," Christopher went on, making his voice deep and mysterious. "The man went first, and the boy followed the man, and if he looked back he saw things with *eyes* coming after him, but he couldn't see what things they were."

"What were they?" asked Robert in a small voice.

"Just things!" said Christopher solemnly. "Spooky things . . . with little red eyes," he added thoughtfully. "Then they came to a clearing place – there was a fire burning – not a yellow fire though, a blue one. All the flames were blue. It looked *ghastly*!" cried Christopher, pleased with his grown-up word. "There were three heads – just heads, no arms or legs or bodies or anything – sticking out of the ground round the fire." He stopped again. Allan and Robert could hear their own breathing. They did not ask any questions and Christopher went on with his story again. "They were ugly, UGLY heads and they had these smiles on their faces" – Christopher was trying to think of words bad enough to describe the smiles – "more horrible than anything you ever saw. They were yellow too, mind you, like cheese. One head looked at the man with cruel, mean eyes and said,

"'So you brought us some food.'

"The man replied, 'Yes, and it's very tender tonight.'

"'Well, it's just as well,' the head said, 'or we'd have to eat *you*.'

"Then the second head said, 'We'll have a good tuck-in tonight, eh, brothers? Bags I be the one to drink his blood.' Then the third head opened its mouth, wide as wide, like a cat yawning, you know, and it had all these pointy teeth, like needles, some short and some long, and it didn't even say anything. It just began to scream, horrible, high-up screams . . ."

Christopher's voice got louder and higher with excitement, and at this very moment, almost it seemed at Robert's ear, a shrill furious howl arose from under the hedge. Allan scrambled to his feet with a cry of terror and went hopping madly out of the tent, too frightened to get out of his sleeping-bag first.

"The head!" yelled Robert and followed him, so frightened he felt sick and shaky in his stomach.

245

Under the hedge were heads with teeth like needles waiting to bite him up as if he was an apple.

Christopher was alone in the tent. Quickly he hopped from under his blankets and stuck his head out through the tent flap. He saw Allan and Robert, still zipped in their sleeping-bags, hopping and stumbling up the lawn.

"It ends happily!" he shouted.

Then he thoughtfully put his hand under Allan's pillow and helped himself to the luncheon sausage hidden there.

Voices were talking on the veranda.

"It was only a cat fight!" Christopher's father was saying. "Great Scott, if you're going to be scared by a cat fight, we'll never make campers of you."

Christopher grinned to himself in the dark and quietly felt for the biscuits under Robert's pillow.

ACKNOWLEDGEMENTS

The publishers wish to thank the following for permission to reproduce copyright material:

Terrance Dicks: "Jekyll and Jane" from *Snake in the Bus and Other Pet Stories*; first published by Methuen Children's Books 1994 and reproduced by permission of The Agency (London) Ltd on behalf of the author. Copyright © Terrence Dicks.

Helen Cresswell: "Double Bluff" from *The Much Better Story Book*; first published by Random House Children's Books 1992 and reproduced by permission of A. M. Heath and Company Ltd on behalf of the author.

Jan Mark: "Mystery Tour" from *Mystery Tour*, ed. Mick Gower; first published by Bodley Head 1991 and reproduced by permission of David Higham Associates on behalf of the author. Copyright © 1991 Jan Mark.

Ian Whybrow: "Sniff Finds a Seagull" from *The Sniff Stories* by Ian Whybrow; first published by Bodley Head 1989 and reproduced by permission of Hodder and Staughton Ltd.

Robert Leeson: "Fun Run" from *Good Sports: A Bag of Sports Stories*, ed. Toby Bradman; first published by Transworld Publishers 1992 and reproduced by permission of the author.

Rory McGrath: "The Man with the Silver Tongue" from *Silver Jackanory*; first published by BBC Books 1991 and reproduced by permission of London Management on behalf of the author.

Richmal Crompton: "William's Busy Day" from *William – The Outlaw* by Richmal Crompton; first published by Macmillan Publishers 1927 and reproduced by permission of A. P. Watt.

Robert Swindells: "You Can't Bring That in Here" from *The Snake on the Bus and Other Stories*; first published by Methuen Children's Books 1994 and reproduced by permission of Jennifer Luithlen Agency on behalf of the author.

Margaret Mahy: "The Horrible Story" from *The Second Margaret Mahy Story Book* by Margaret Mahy; first published by Orion Children's Books 1972 and reproduced by permission of Orion Publishing Group Ltd.

Margaret Mahy: "A Work of Art" from *The Door in the Air and Other Stories* by Margaret Mahy; first published by Orion Children's Books and reproduced by permission of Orion Publishing Group Ltd.

ACKNOWLEDGEMENTS

Norman Hunter: "Burglars" from *The Incredible Adventures of Professor Branestawm* by Norman Hunter; first published by Bodley Head and reproduced by permission of Random House UK Ltd.

Janet Francis Smith: "Sticky Bun and the Sandwich Challenge" from *The Independent Story of the Year*, 1988, and reproduced by permission of Scholastic Ltd.

Hazel Townson: "Murder by Omelette" from *Love Them, Hate Them*, ed. Tony Bradman; first published by Methuen Children's Books 1991 and reproduced by permission of the author.

Peter Dickinson: "Barker"; reproduced by permission of A. P. Watt on behalf of the author.

Terry Tapp: "The Day I Died" reproduced by permission of the author.

Every effort has been made to trace the copyright holders but where this has not been possible or where any error has been made the publishers will be pleased to make the necessary arrangement at the first opportunity.

Books in this series available from Macmillan

The prices shown below are correct at the time of going to press. However, Macmillan Publishers reserve the right to show new retail prices on covers which may differ from those previously advertised.

Funny Stories for Six Year Olds	0 330 36857 5	£3.99
Magical Stories for Six Year Olds	0 330 36858 3	£3.99
Animal Stories for Six Year Olds	0 330 36859 1	£3.99
Funny Stories for Seven Year Olds	0 330 34945 7	£3.99
Scary Stories for Seven Year Olds	0 330 34943 0	£3.99
Animal Stories for Seven Year Olds	0 330 35494 9	£3.99
Funny Stories for Eight Year Olds	0 330 34946 5	£3.99
Scary Stories for Eight Year Olds	0 330 34944 9	£3.99
Animal Stories for Eight Year Olds	0 330 35495 7	£3.99
Funny Stories for Nine Year Olds	0 330 37491 5	£3.99
Scary Stories for Nine Year Olds	0 330 37492 3	£3.99
Animal Stories for Nine Year Olds	0 330 37493 1	£3.99

All Macmillan titles can be ordered at your local bookshop or are available by post from:

**Book Service by Post
PO Box 29, Douglas, Isle of Man IM99 1BQ**

Credit cards accepted. For details:
Telephone: 01624 675137
Fax: 01624 670923
E-mail: bookshop@enterprise.net

Free postage and packing in the UK.
Overseas customers: add £1 per book (paperback)
and £3 per book (hardback).